Chinese Opera

… that irremediable space
between performance and consequence,
between trailing images of the same person
framed moments apart, at once magnificent and insignificant.

Chinese Opera

Alex Kuo

Asia 2000 Limited
Hong Kong

ISBN 962-7160-59-8

Published by Asia 2000 Ltd
1101 Seabird House,
22–28 Wyndham Street, Central,
Hong Kong

http://www.asia2000.com.hk/

Typeset with Ventura Publisher in Adobe Garamond by Asia 2000
Printed in Hong Kong by Regal Printing
First printing 1998

For Ken, who completely changed my music;
and for Joan, who listens with delight.

I just want you to get my damn history straight, it matters to me.
— Jessica Hagedorn, *Dogeaters*

We do history in the morning and change it after lunch.
— Don DeLillo, *Mao II*

One

THE STORY BEGINS with Sissy going to China in January 1989, the Year of the Snake. But then it's not her story; Sissy's only one part of it.

Sissy told me about her involvement in it, and since then I've spent most of two years putting the rest of its parts together: I've eavesdropped on whispers with my Nagra microphone, hatched questions, looked behind gestures; many nights my telephone hummed with conversation, and my fax machine received urgent and sometimes sinister messages; interviews were arranged with belligerent under-secretaries of immigration, archivists of birth records, alumni gatekeepers; I've mapped an entire topography from old driving records and bank accounts, looked up retired postal carriers, tricksters, insurance brokers; spent a January in frigid Changchun on the trail of a disappeared person; and once even tried to get into the underground vaults of the Mormon Redemption Center. In short, in these two years I've collected everything tangible and transcribable on both sides of the Pacific.

Even though I am not in this story, in a way I feel I've always been in it as an unseen observer, because I can't think of a better story to be watching. But you see, it's not all that simple and clear-cut.

You'll see no more of me until the end of this story, but I can't promise you won't see my hand here and there soldering a disruptive seam, discarding some evidence inconsequential to the narrative, inserting an interpretation, or embellishing a dialogue *poco poco.*

You've got to trust me a little here because, and believe me, I've got a lot more to lose than you. It's my career as an essential informant that's on the line here, and it's also my acquired reconstructed history that you're looking at, no lie. You've got to agree to that at least.

When Sister was in gradeschool her schoolmates taunted her during recess by calling her *Sissy;* but a few years later she saw the imperative in keeping that nickname when she started developing an interest in boys, and has ever since tried to publicly deny the legal name in her birth certificate and passport. That passport was now balanced on her lap with her purse, so she could copy its number onto the customs declaration form. *Sister George.* It was one of many of her mother's lifelong little errors in naming, after having conceived her in the back of a weathered pickup truck on that wild night thirty-nine years ago parked at some backwater inlet where twelve years later the Wanapum Dam, named after her father's tribe would stretch across the Columbia River. Sissy had not sought legal alteration of her name, but had accepted it as a necessary reminder of her origins in those private moments when it was important that she remembered, even though her driver's license, credit cards, checks and other identification had always discreetly presented her as *Sissy George.*

"You American?" asked the man in the window seat, looking over at Sissy's blue passport. He had waited four hours until they were almost over Beijing from Tokyo before finally asking what he had wanted to know when she first sat down next to him.

"Yes," she looked up and smiled, but quickly returned her attention to the customs form.

Both of them felt the slow, grinding lowering of the heavy landing gear of the 747. The man looked out the window, but Sissy knew that he was only formulating the best question to satisfy his curiosity. She'd been through this with men before in places in her own country where she had performed, Hartford, Kansas City, Boulder.

The 747 continued its long and lumbering descent.

"I think you Mongolian, tall, but your skin too dark. What do you do?"

"I'm a singer," Sissy slipped her passport back into her purse which she placed on the empty seat between them.

She fidgeted with her pen and thought that as long as he continued with this double cipher, he'd never find out. At this point he's too blown away by her answer to even ask the right questions.

"You come sing in China?"

"No, I'm visiting a friend from America." Sissy looked down and continued with the form.

US$425 cash. *No* gold or silver jewelry. *No* camera. Sony Walkman, $150. *No* video camera. *Yes* printed matter, but it didn't ask what. *No* antiques, goods and samples, and recorded video tape. *Yes* two months of withheld affection from my partner.

Just as Sissy was unbuckling her seatbelt to quickly go to the lavatory before the final descent, the man to her left turned and spoke to her again.

"I hope you enjoy China," he ventured a smile.

Sissy thought that he had said this in sincerity, and was embarrassed by her earlier reflex reaction of racial suspicion.

"Thank you," she said, smiling back, wishing she could remember the words among the few she had learned in her Chinese phrase book. "Thank you."

She changed her mind about brushing her teeth and combing her hair, and asked instead, "Are you, are you returning to China?"

He looked at her and hesitated.

"I am going home. I not like Australia," he added deliberately. "Here is my card."

He reached into his suit pocket for his wallet and lifted a gilt-edged business card.

"Here," he said, "I am going home."

"Thanks," Sissy reached across the empty seat for it.

Luo Zhiquan, Associate Professor of Mathematics, Tsinghua University, Beijing.

"I'm afraid I don't have a card. But my name is Sissy George, and I'll be in Beijing too."

"Sissy, Sissy Jor?"

"No," she laughed and threw her head back. "It's George, G, E, O, R, G, E, like the boy's name, but quite a common last name in central and eastern Washington state, my father's family name."

Here she stopped and looked past him out the cabin window, thinking about the only time she had ever seen her father, about ten years ago when she went to look for him, there fishing alone for steelhead above the bridge at Monitor.

"I am sorry. Sissy George."

It was the fifth day in a row that Sissy had driven to the end of this dirt road in a rented car. Twice a day, once in the early morning and once in the late afternoon, she would get out, light a cigarette, and walk the last half-mile to the point where the Wenatchee River temporarily divided around a tall boulder. Then she would pick out a rock to sit on, looking as much as a mile up and down the river for her father, because her mother had told her what he had said that wild — and only — night she'd met him in Ellensburg. Ever since he was seven, he'd fish for steelhead every spring and every fall at land's tip just above the Monitor bridge.

Every day for four days Sissy had sat under the late October sun and looked for hours into the water, upriver and then down, to her left and then to her right, for some figure to suddenly emerge from either shadow or bright sunshine, some glint of light from a fishing rod's ferric joints as it quavered in its overhead cast. On the second day she saw a round, black shape just at the last bend and ripple upriver that she could see. It was moving toward her at the same speed as the water, and squinting into the late afternoon sunlight, shading her eyes with her hand, she could soon see a shimmer of light, and soon that it was attached to a moving purplish shape lilting down river with the water, a thin dark arm attached to the dark mass.

It was a man fishing the river in an inner tube, and by the time he was within what Sissy imagined was a quickly-receding hailing distance, he waved at her with his hand from which hung circlets of free line. By the time Sissy had absorbed all of this and waved back, the fisherman had already passed her on the outer side of the river's separation.

On the next day a black bear emerged from the shadows of the bank opposite her and splashed into the river. Sissy got up when it seemed that the bear was swimming straight for her tip of land, but it saw her in time, snorted above the noise of the thin rapids, turned its head and completed its crossing against the current upstream and away from her.

Yesterday she was beginning to believe her serious doubts about finding her father out here. After all, she told herself, his story had been told to her mother almost forty years ago, and anything can happen in that time, anything can change. Maybe she had the details wrong, or maybe her mother had remembered the details wrong or had changed some of them when Sissy, with a freshly-minted voice diploma from Indiana tucked in her purse five years ago, asked her mother for the first time in her life, for stories about her father whom she'd never seen, not even a picture.

But she decided she would stay at least until the end of the week, she had waited so long to come so far. And anyway, she had no other story to believe in.

And besides that, the river had by now become a presence in her life. Each day each detail had become more familiar to her, each rock face that she sat on, the distance to the ripples and darker beyond even in the morning sun behind her, and above that the apple and pear orchards rising in tiered segments out of the earth on both sides of the river, and beyond that the quick rise of bedrock walls the color of desert dust until they reached their escarpments and stretched beyond the dark brown of Sissy's eye.

Each night back at the motel, her dreams were filled with these details, as if she were living her life twice, except that in her dreams' second life, there was more to see and more to understand and remember. In them she heard the noise of the rippling splash of water in front of her and the hum of logging and beer truck tires on the highway a mile away against the rhythmic flow of the river and the occasional strident click of a nearby grasshopper. Here she saw the distant hills dotted with tall red ponderosas, and high above them once, the dissipating cloud from a silent jet's vapor trail. Here in one dream she remembered that seventeen thousand years ago Lake Missoula broke, and in looking for a way to the Pacific, it reshaped and redefined everything in its path, right down to that smooth rock she had sat on that day, the stunted firs that would grow here almost in defiance, the bear that would find its home here, and now Sissy who'd come to find her father here.

"You are waiting for me," a man's voice said.

Neither startled nor surprised, Sissy turned her head toward the river, as she had expected. He was walking slowly towards her, balancing his rod in one hand and tackle box and large net in the other, looking his way over the rocks and at her at the same time.

Sissy said nothing.

He appeared darker than Sissy had imagined, and a bit shorter, but younger. Yet none of this made any difference when he reached the boulder she was leaning against.

"It's been a long time," he said.

"Yes," Sissy smiled. "Yes, I know. I'm very lucky."

"We're both very lucky."

Sissy's father took a moment to set down his gear and rod on a flat rock before continuing. Sissy saw that his hands moved deliberately, used to being careful with everything.

"Some stories that are true never change. I have thought many times about you. When I've flicked the lure into the water, I have thought with certainty that our lives would one day come to this here."

The two of them together looked away into the distance and leaned back against the same boulder, breathing in the same clear air, shaped in that space between river and desert.

"I'm very happy here," Sissy said, reaching for his hand.

"Just like your mother's, but lighter," he said, looking at her hand. "Are you also a singer?"

"Yes, but it's jazz, not country."

"Just as well, *enit.* That country singing got her into a lot of trouble. Even now it's not safe for her here," he said, pointing down river towards Wenatchee.

In this way they spent the rest of the day. When it started to get dark, they went to his pickup truck and returned with two sleeping bags, a baloney and cheese sandwich, and apples and beer.

And within this night, it appeared to them that it never got dark, that their voices found for each other in low tones what each wanted to know about their lives apart and the stories they had inhabited up to now, and until Sissy told me this, she had never used the word *share,* and would not thereafter either.

Sissy must have fallen asleep. When she woke up, her father had built a small fire from the river's debris on which were resting a steaming blackened coffee pot and a darker, wrought-iron pan with two browned trout in it.

When it was time to leave, Sissy walked down to the water's edge where her father was reeling in his line. She looked at him and could feel his presence and what she wanted to say, but she could not find the words. So she just stood there and touched his arm.

"Be careful with yourself Sissy, you are the only one of us left," her father said, and turned back toward the river.

Inside the Beijing airport terminal, lines were quickly forming for customs inspection. Sissy slowed down and looked at the BLUE, GREEN and RED markers and saw that the longest lines were formed for the RED.

"You go GREEN," Professor Luo said behind her, struggling with his five carry-ons.

"But I've got declared items, my Walkman and some music scores," Sissy turned, surprised that he was right behind her with his load.

"No matter, you American," Professor Luo smiled, rushing off to the shortest RED line. He turned and added, "See you again."

In the direction past Professor Luo, she saw her friend Sonny with his shoulder-length hair, steadily waving both wrists above his head, the same way that he sometimes physically warmed up before starting a serious practice session on the piano.

Two

TIRED FROM ARGUING with the chair of the department all morning, Sonny returned to his apartment and took a nap.

In his dream he was the exiled son of China's revolution, the latest version of the modern revolution that killed his mother when he was four. Almost half a century later he had returned to lead a life of dissidence in Beijing, secretly but diligently leading his students to complete the task unfinished by Mao in 1949. There were many meetings in his apartment, and in one of them a student composed a poem for this cause to defeat the three mountains of feudalism, imperialism and bureaucratic capitalism.

Then the dream shifted to the television footage of a CNN reporter covering their heroic ascent up a snow-covered peak, followed by students with banners streaming, workers, farmers, and in the rear, China's best, the intelligentsia. But wait, the mountain was transforming. It was Kilimanjaro, no, it was McKinley, no, it was Fuji: it had become all of them.

". . . Sonny . . ."

He could feel the straps of the oxygen tank slipping off the nylon shoulders of his expedition jacket.

". . . Sonny, Sonny, wake up."

It was the voice of the student who had written the poem, his graduate piano student, and she was bent over him, gently shaking his nearer shoulder.

"What is it Liyuan?"

Sonny sat up and swung his legs over the side of the bed, registering that he had slept most of the afternoon, and it was now already early evening.

"You were shouting. You were dreaming," she straightened up and tossed her hair back.

Sonny quickly looked around to get his bearings, and saw his cassettes and tapes on the windowsill, music scores on the dresser and the floor, and a rolled-up yellow copy of Chopin's *Études* in Liyuan's hand. He recognized this as his apartment in the three weeks since Christmas that he'd been in Beijing.

"What are you doing here?"

"I knocked. But you were shouting, so I came in. The door was not locked."

Sonny got up and flipped on the light and showed her into the living room.

"No, I mean, why did you come here?"

"Oh, sorry," Liyuan blushed. "I was practicing and want your advice on fingering."

"Please sit," Sonny waved to a chair. "Some tea?"

"Oh no, I don't want to trouble you."

"No trouble, just some green tea?"

Sonny went into the narrow kitchen but found the tea tin empty. He held it upside down and shook it.

"Look, empty. I'm sorry."

"No matter. We heard you arguing with Professor Zhou this morning."

"But you must sign contract," Madame Zhou insisted again.

"Madame Zhou, I won't sign it. Before I came, the former chair said I would be teaching piano and music theory, not music history, and giving a recital." Sonny was adamant. "Look," he added, "there's his letter in your hand."

Madame Zhou had not looked at the letter since Sonny, the visiting Chinese American hotshot pianist, handed it to her over half an hour ago. Secretly she despised the former chair who was always sucking up to the vice-president. Now he'd been rewarded with a trip to research music programs in America on state money, a rubbish project, and she had to clean up after him. She was also resentful that she had been asked to come out of semi-retirement to do his job, make up for his follies and amend his lies. She carefully set the letter down on her score-littered desk and picked up a pencil to emphasize her argument.

"To get salary next week, you must sign contract," Madame Zhou waved her pencil.

Sonny shifted a little. The two of them had been at this for more than an hour, doubling back, skipping, rushing forward, only to double back again.

"But I want to teach theory. I didn't bring my notes or tapes for music history," Sonny said, emphasizing *music history* as if they were dirty words, or worst, bourgeoisie words.

Sonny heard his own words and thought that they sounded weak. But then he also thought that Madame Zhou was also taking a position which she did not personally believe either. The fact that he had participated in this exchange for so long made him suspect that he was more Chinese than he'd thought.

Madame Zhou got up and prepared two cups of tea with hot water from her thermos. She offered Sonny one across the desk with the hand with the crushed fingers.

"The students need history," she started again.

"I've talked with my studio students, and I believe they need theory."

"Our library has tapes and books for history."

"What do you have against theory?"

"Perhaps I don't," Madame said, looking out past the plants on her windowsill. "But the students must have history."

"Madame Zhou Nianci, as leader of the department, can't you make an exception this once?"

"No, that is not possible. They have no need for theory. Theory is bourgeois. Our students need to have only one theory, that which surrounds them every moment of their lives. It is easier for them: they do not have to ask why; all their questions already answered before them. They need only history."

Shocked by her honesty, Sonny could not find the right words.

"And whose version of, of, history must I teach?"

With this last question, Sonny thought again that his position was weakening in this minor argument against Madame Zhou, the most distinguished and dignified piano teacher in all of China who had ended her own performing career when she crushed her left fingers moving a grand piano by herself during the Cultural Revolution, someone who had been listened to and instantly obeyed without question for almost half a century, since before Sonny was born. Already he was toying with the idea of teaching Western music history in China.

"It does not matter, as long as we think you are teaching history. Twenty years ago, in 1969, we taught history with nothing, nothing at all. All the musical instruments in Beijing, both Western and Chinese, were destroyed by the Red Guards in the first week of their revolution. When the school reopened in late 1969, we did not have time to repair enough pianos for classroom demonstration — we sang and hummed everything."

So that's it, Sonny thought, but since he had persevered the two hours into this argument, he decided to go further with it.

"But your music library is very incomplete. There are simply not enough recordings for a proper music history course."

"No matter. I have heard you play. You can do it with the piano."

Sonny wanted to give it one more try, but he knew that he had already conceded.

"I can't do everything on the piano. Franz Liszt tried with his transcriptions, heaven knows, but they didn't work and today nobody but that crazy Canadian plays them anymore, and then only in a New York recording studio. But you know, things like oboes, reed instruments, how do I do them on the piano?"

"Mr. Ling, have you tried placing cloth over the strings?" Madame Zhou suggested with only the slightest hint of triumph in her voice. "We Chinese have learned to do with what we have, not bemoan what we have lost or what we don't have."

After Sonny signed his contract, the two of them left the building together and walked toward Fuxingmennei.

"Mr. Ling," Madame Zhou said when they had stopped at a street crossing, "I know you cannot teach history without theory."

Sonny looked at her, but did not know how to respond to her smile.

"Are you used to this weather?" Madame Zhou stopped just before they separated, her smile gone.

"Yes," Sonny answered, his voice changed since leaving the conservatory. "In Chicago it's much colder, with the wind off the lake."

"Wind will come here to Beijing too, later this spring."

After Sonny had suggested two different fingerings for the left hand for Liyuan's assigned Chopin étude, during which he thought that she wasn't particularly attentive, they sat back in their chairs in the living room and avoided looking at each other. Sonny was growing impatient, he wanted the space to focus on what his dreams might have meant. He wished for Sissy, she'd know what they meant.

"How much do you practice?" Sonny asked.

"Perhaps I must go now," Liyuan said, fastening the buttons of her overcoat that she had kept on during the entire conference.

In the three weeks of negotiating his way around Beijing, Sonny had become used to the directive meaning of the adverb *perhaps,* and he saw this as a chance to try it out himself.

"Perhaps yes," he said, but he knew it had not come out right.

Liyuan got up and Sonny walked her to the top of the stairs and waved goodbye.

Right after he had made sure that the apartment door lock had clicked into place, he thought he heard three light knocks on the door. He stood and waited, anticipating something he was not prepared to confront. After the second three light taps, Sonny slowly opened the door.

"May I come in?" Liyuan asked, taking a step forward, looking up at Sonny.

"But it's getting late," Sonny said, stepping back.

"I want to stay tonight," Liyuan said, looking away.

"No. No you can't," Sonny looked at her. Since he heard no conviction in his voice, he added, "The compound guard will know and report us. There'll be trouble."

"No, he does not know, he did not see me come in."

"But you can't, you're my student. . . ."

Liyuan threw herself at Sonny and hugged him. Sonny found her hair under his nose, and his hands moved cautiously to patting and rubbing the back of her down-stuffed overcoat, ever careful not to send the wrong signal. He felt what he supposed were Liyuan's feigned sobs, and wondered if she had been sent to test his part of the contract he had signed this morning in Madame Zhou's office.

"You can't stay, they'll know no matter, we'll both get into big trouble. Like Berlin or Hollywood, you know, everybody knows everything that happens here, but for different reasons. They'll deport me. We'll start an international incident, and they'll send you to who knows where."

Sonny could only feel Liyuan hold on tighter.

"Listen, Liyuan. . . ." Sonny said.

He was determined not to lose his second argument in the same day to another Chinese woman, and hoped Liyuan was not from the same province that Madame Zhou was from, where they must raise their women to be tough and win all arguments, especially against men.

"Listen Liyuan. . . ." Sonny tried again.

He wanted to say, *With your uneven eyes, you're just on the edge of beauty,* and *It isn't that you're not attractive,* but he was worried his meaning would be lost in her translation. So instead he said, "Liyuan, I am too old for you. I want to be your teacher. I can't be your teacher if I'm also your lover."

"I do not want to make love," Liyuan said and slightly released her embrace. "I only want to sleep with you one night."

31

Before he realized that he was confused by Liyuan's ambiguity, or that she was also confused by it, Sonny continued with his argument.

"Liyuan, students do not sleep with their teachers. And besides, I have a fiancée," he exaggerated, glad to find another reason. "She's a singer, and she's coming to Beijing next week."

"Is she American?" Liyuan asked, loosening her clutch. Sonny imagined her face as capable of suddenly falling apart in the intensity of lovemaking.

"Yes, yes she is, more than most."

"Sorry," Liyuan released Sonny. "I mean is she Chinese?"

"No, but what do you mean?" Sonny sounded impatient.

In one quick motion, Liyuan left Sonny and rushed out the door.

"See you tomorrow at the lesson," Sonny trailed after her at the top of the stairs.

By then Liyuan had already turned onto the lower landing and was gone.

Three

THEY HAD SQUEEZED OUT of the airport together, the two of them, and stood in line for their turn at a taxi, still balancing Sissy's luggage and trying to touch each other and talk all at the same time. It all seemed very unreal to Sissy, who only moments ago was more than half a day behind and almost nine thousand miles away hurriedly filling out her luggage tags at a ticket counter at O'Hare. Now some twenty hours later, her eyes were adjusting to the complicated landscape around the Beijing airport.

"This is pretty incredible," she said. "One moment I'm on Jackson trying to find a scarf and score for you, and next I'm in Tokyo, and before I even got to find my way around Narita, I'm in Beijing."

"It's so good to see you," Sonny smiled at her, saying it again and adding, "I've really missed you."

"How's your Chinese coming along?"

"We'll find out in a moment here."

The cabby asked Sonny their destination while tucking Sissy's luggage into the trunk.

"Women chu yin daxiwei," Sonny answered.

"Shenme?"

"Yin da xi wei," Sonny repeated, slower and louder this time.

The driver only looked more perplexed.

"This is not working," Sonny said to a laughing Sissy. Then to the driver, "Beijing Hotel."

"Ah, Beijing Hotel, *hao, hao,* okay."

"Sonny," Sissy said after they were in the cab. "Sonny, why are we going to a hotel?"

They were driving down the wide boulevards lined with willows and elms spaced evenly apart, and Sissy noticed an unusual mix of traffic that included Mercedes, agricultural trucks, bicycles and horse-drawn carts.

"It's close to the music school, and I can direct him from there."

"Ah, music school, near Beijing Hotel. I know, I know, *Xinwenhua Jie,"* the driver acknowledged and turned his eyes back to the road.

Sissy looked at Sonny, the corners of her mouth rising into a smile.

"I've only been here five weeks, Sissy, give me a break," he said, and joined Sissy in her laughter.

"But you're supposed to be Chinese," Sissy continued laughing.

"Then you haven't looked close enough," Sonny smiled, showing his teeth.

A little bit breathless after climbing the stairs, Sonny set down the bags inside the apartment door.

"This is it," he said, and took Sissy's hand to show her the rest of the large two-room-and-bath apartment.

"This is huge, Sonny, this is great," she said, holding out her other hand toward Sonny.

The late afternoon sun was brightening up the living room, and the two of them walked over to the window together.

"Looks like another postcard sunset, an illusion created by Beijing's pollution," Sonny said behind Sissy, putting both arms around her.

Sissy turned into his kiss, pushing herself into him, as if she had no bones.

"I've missed you too," she whispered.

Sonny started pressing his hands against her clothes and was surprised to find that he could not feel her body at all.

"What all you wearing here?" he asked.

"You guess okay?"

He took off both their coats and hung them up in the clothes tree in the hallway.

"I'm having my period," Sissy hesitated.

"When has that made any difference?"

Into the bedroom and onto the bed, Sonny pulled her behind him. There he held her face and kissed her on the mouth and then her cheeks and then her eyes. She rolled Sonny over, cradling her head into his arm and touching his chest with her free hand. Sonny reached down under her arm and several layers of shirts, and then Sissy could feel her nipples hardening as he slowly traced her breasts under his opened palm.

Then there was Sissy's clothing, Sonny's hand fumbling at the complications.

Next, three light knocks on the apartment door.

"Sonny, did you lock it?"

"Yes, but I must answer."

"Sonny!"

"I must; they know we're here. Everyone knows everything that goes on here."

They got up, and Sonny waited until Sissy had smoothed down her clothes before opening the door.

The foreign affairs office director of the Central Conservatory of Music stood there with his short military haircut and wire-framed glasses, a plastic bag of oranges in one hand and his hat and gloves in the other.

"Come in, come in," Sonny said. "We just got here from the airport."

"Yes I know. I just want to welcome your friend."

"Oh Yes," Sonny said and introduced him.

"I welcome you here," he said and gave Sissy the bag of oranges.

He reached into his coat pocket and got out a business card.

"I hope you enjoy Beijing and our school," Chang Feng Qi said as he handed Sissy his card.

"Thank you very much."

"Wouldn't you like to have a cup of tea?" Sonny asked, and saw a slight glint in Sissy's eyes that only he understood.

"No, you must be busy," Chang said, stepping back. "I will leave now."

They followed Chang to the top of the stairs.

"You are famous singer," Chang turned to Sissy. "Perhaps you will sing for us."

"Oh no, I'm not famous, but I'll sing for you sometime," Sissy answered and then arched an eyebrow toward Sonny.

"What was that about?" Sissy continued when they were back in the bedroom.

"Oh, Chang. Chang was just being hospitable."

"I don't mean that. I mean the famous part. Sonny, what have you told them?"

"Nothing, Sissy, just that you are my partner and that you're a singer."

"Oh yeah?" Sissy said and propped herself on an elbow on the bed. "And what else?"

"And that you've been in several operas and musicals since you were in highschool, and that you make your living now singing vocal backup for an LA recording studio and working jazz spots around the country and examining me."

"That makes me famous?"

By now Sonny was on his elbow too.

"There're some words that have different meanings here. *Famous* seems to describe anything that's out of the ordinary."

Sonny reached a hand toward her, but Sissy seemed distracted.

"What's that?" she asked.

"What's what?"

Then he too heard it, another three light knocks on the door.

"For chrissake Sonny, don't they believe people have a sex life here?"

"Not since one child per couple became national policy in 1979," he sighed, getting up again to open the door.

Madame Zhou had also come to welcome Sissy, and had brought along a bowl of narcissus bulbs about to bloom.

"Madame Zhou, how nice of you to come. This is Sissy," Sonny waved toward his companion who was brushing back some hair from her eyes.

"This is for you," Madame Zhou said smiling, giving Sissy the bowl. "Welcome you to Beijing and our Spring Festival."

"Thank you so much. Spring Festival?"

"Yes, new Chinese Lunar Year, in a week. Year of Snake."

Madame Zhou had also come to invite them for dinner the next day at her apartment.

Madame Zhou and Zheng Xiaomei had been preparing dinner all afternoon in Madame's tiny kitchen, chatting and enjoying what they were doing. By the time the guests arrived, everything was ready, the living room filled with the lingering fragrance of narcissus blossoms and incense.

Sonny and Sissy were the first to knock on the door just before Chang, and Madame Zhou introduced the Americans to Zheng.

"This is Zheng Xiaomei, my good friend who sometimes teaches opera conducting at our conservatory."

"You mean *the* Zheng Xiaomei, *the* Zheng Xiaomei who studied with Bain in Moscow?" Sissy asked, her eyes astonished.

"Yes. My English not good as Russian," Zheng smiled and held out her braceleted hand. "You Sissy George, jazz singer, Madame Zhou told me. *Ni hao*, Chang. And you, Sonny Ling.

My friend she said you excellent pianist. She must know. And you teach our students piano."

"And music history," Sonny said and looked at Madame Zhou, and they both laughed.

Sissy had not moved since shaking Zheng's hand, and continued to stare at her, her lips parted — she was still awed by the reality that she had just been introduced to someone she had heard and read about at Indiana, a legend who as a student had conducted a symphony in the Kremlin Theater in the early sixties, who then became the first woman conductor to raise her baton in the Moscow Musical Theater with *Tosca,* and who later received France's Medal of Honor for Art for being the first person to direct Bizet's *Carmen* in China. Sissy thought that Zheng must be over fifty, but in her short, short hair cropped around her face and arched eyebrows, she looked about her own age.

"Sissy, Sissy," Sonny interrupted. "Take off your shoes. Here, wear these slippers."

Two conversations were going on at once. Sissy wanted to know more about Zheng, and Sonny was discussing his upcoming recital program with Madame Zhou.

"What will you play for recital?"

"And then what happened to you during the Cultural Revolution?"

"I thought I'd start with Schumann's *Kreisleriana*," Sonny's chopsticks fidgeted with the shrimp dumpling on his plate.

"Oh Mr. Chang," Sissy looked across the table at him. "I hope you're not bored by all this shop talk."

"And what for second half?" Madame Zhou looked suspiciously at Sonny.

"Not at all. I enjoy music. I studied voice here years ago."

"This is a great dinner, Madame Zhou, thank you," Sonny said, putting down his chopsticks.

"And thanks to my old friend here," Madame Zhou nodded to Zheng. "She is better cook."

Then, looking straight at Sonny, she added, "What after intermission?"

"In Cultural Revolution I sent to army. But I not waste time. I taught soldiers singing, one whole year *The Yellow River Cantata*. And, and," Zheng paused and laughed, looking first at Madame Zhou and then Sonny, "I composed a piano concerto on *Internationale.*"

"I thought I'd follow the Schumann with Liszt's *Mazeppa* study of revenge before the intermission."

Sissy stopped in mid-sentence and turned to look at Sonny; Zheng also turned her head and raised her arched eyebrows further. No one said anything. Chang, the only one at the table who could not follow the details, looked down in embarrassment. Sonny finally picked up his chopsticks and placed the shrimp dumpling in his mouth.

Madame Zhou broke the silence and laughed and said to Sonny for all of them, "You are lunatic."

In the diminishing laughter, she added, "And what after that?"

Relieved, Zheng returned to her conversation with Sissy.

"And then I did *Carmen* with Central Opera and Ballet four years ago. In French. We rehearsing again for April," Zheng added, looking carefully at Sissy.

"I've thought about Beethoven's Opus III," Sonny reached for another shrimp dumpling. "These are great."

"What after?"

"Hah, hah, Mr. Ling. What will you follow that with, *Goldberg Variations?*"

"Canberra, Rome, some Western, some Chinese, some opera, some ballet, sometimes both in the same month."

Sissy heard Madame Zhou say that Sonny's program was impossible, too difficult and too heavy and too long for the Beijing audience that wanted to get home before nine, but he responded by suggesting switching around the Schumann and the Liszt.

"And what do you mean the Beijing audience? Won't it be for the conservatory audience?" Sonny looked at Madame Zhou.

"No. You are better pianist. We have Beijing Concert Hall. Their piano better. You can choose Steinway or new Bosendorfer."

Sissy saw that Sonny had stopped talking, and was gazing absently at Zheng.

"And you, Sissy," Zheng asked. "Have you been happy with your work?"

Here the discussions went back to their separate ways again.

"So Madame Zhou, so you want something simpler, some *Reader's Digest* program, light, short pieces?"

"Yes, very much. I've enjoyed doing my work. It's been much better since I stopped smoking a couple years ago. Now I do the jazz that I love at night-clubs, and the recording backup in Los Angeles more than pays the rent."

"No, I am not stupid," Madame Zhou answered. "Your program impossible anywhere. Perhaps we discuss later."

"You can enjoy your music. You very lucky Sissy George," Zheng said.

The lights on Chang'an Boulevard glittered in the light snowfall when Sonny and Sissy walked back to the foreigners' guesthouse inside the music school compound. They both had expected a relaxing dinner in which superficial views on

China and the United States would be exchanged without consequence and everyone would have marveled at how China has eliminated homelessness and hunger in just forty years; but instead they encountered a challenging and exhilarating evening which left them feeling both relief and regret now that it was over.

"What an evening. Great. Nobody asked if both my parents were Chinese and why I don't know the language. Nobody stared at you wondering if your mother was a slave and if your father had killed George Armstrong Custer."

"And then meeting the legendary Zheng Xiaomei. I still can't believe it. That Madame Zhou's some tough lady," Sissy continued, reaching for Sonny's hand. "She reminds me of the Hobbema women I've heard about up in Alberta."

"What Hobbema women?" Sonny pulled back Sissy's arm to let some cars pass before crossing Chang'an.

"They're Crees, up in Alberta."

"Oh. You seem to have made friends with Zheng Xiaomei."

"Would you believe it? There she was a perfect jewel!"

"And are you a perfect jewel tonight?"

Sissy smiled and bumped him with her hips.

"How old d'you think she looks?"

"I'd say forty"

"I thought so too, but she's got to be close to sixty."

Four

SHE'S PREGNANT! Four months into rehearsals and she told her director that she was four months pregnant.

"Director Zheng, I am not married," she added, her eyes reflecting both hesitancy and defiance.

Zheng Xiaomei looked at the lead singer carefully, and she felt envy, anger and alarm, in that order. She imagined that most women in this same situation would be in tears at this moment, but her Carmen appeared to be asking for neither advice nor consent. Never having developed any sympathy for romantic love or its consequences, Xiaomei shifted her concentration to finding a rational solution.

"What are you going to do?" she asked, thinking that she should have asked herself that same question.

"Perhaps my boyfriend will come back from Hong Kong in May."

"What does that mean?"

"I will have the baby in May."

Xiaomei looked at her and tried to imagine the shape of her body beneath her clothes, and then ahead in four months to the May performance, projecting the same small shape now muddled by the materials of her overcoat, grown into a large and noticeable dome prohibiting the leaps and dancing demanded by the role of Carmen.

"Can you have both?" Xiaomei tried to say it for her. "Can you have both the baby and Carmen?" she added impatiently.

"Oh no, impossible. I am very sorry."

Having been equally rebellious all her life, Xiaomei did not feel the necessity to ask why her Carmen dared to be different, why she didn't wait until marriage like all the others, and why now, in the middle of a production.

Later when she was alone, Xiaomei looked at her marked and frayed score of *Carmen,* then picked up the phone to call Sissy for lunch.

"She's pregnant?" Sissy repeated.

"Yes, four months."

They were having lunch at Xiaomei's apartment, the sound of an occasional Spring Festival firecracker outside the building marking their conversation.

"And she's not married? I didn't think that sort of thing was supposed to happen in China. What's she going to do, have an abortion?"

"No, but many women do."

"I see."

Xiaomei raised an eyebrow and looked at Sissy, giving nothing away.

Sissy stared back, the hard understanding between their eyes propelling them forward.

"You're not! You're not thinking," Sissy flustered, shifted in her chair, dropped her chopsticks and leaned back.

Xiaomei was silent, looking down at the table.

"But I haven't sung that kind of thing in years," Sissy protested. "Or done that kind of demanding dancing. I'm too old for it now."

"You have sung *Carmen* before, and we both know the dancing in this one is easy."

"Yes, but that was six years ago last. There must be someone else," Sissy pleaded.

"Yes, but I want you," Xiaomei said, finally looking up at Sissy. "You are perfect for it."

"But you're five months into rehearsals already. How about just singing in the chorus?"

"No. There are always singers in world for that. Cape Town. Bismarck. Liverpool. Rio. Here, Beijing," Xiaomei waved around the room.

"You haven't even heard me sing."

"I know singers, and I have heard you humming," Xiaomei said gently. "Warm, lusty mezzo-soprano."

Xiaomei risked arresting a developing friendship, but she was convinced that Sissy was perfect for the part that she wanted as director of the opera.

"God!" Sissy exclaimed, setting down her chopsticks again. "I don't even know more than ten words of Chinese."

"No matter. We are doing *Carmen* in original, French. It does not matter. We all do Italian, Spanish, German, but we do not know their meaning. No matter on stage," Xiaomei guaranteed, pausing to let a string of firecrackers take its course.

"Do not worry," she continued. "You will have a prompter for help."

"I don't believe this," Sissy nearly stammered, getting up from the table and moving to the piano bench. "I don't believe that you've just asked me, an American crossblood, to sing in French in China the faked-Spanish music of a Frenchman who'd refused to go to Spain. You'll really have to give the tickets away now, like the first time *Carmen* was produced at the Opéra-Comique. This certainly puts a new crimp into the meaning of multiculturalism. And I don't believe that I'm even thinking seriously of doing it."

"Next she'll ask me to do a Chinese opera," Sissy said to Bizet's score on the music stand next to the piano.

"You are already in one," Xiaomei smiled. "Perhaps this will have happy ending. *Carmen* has long history in China. Few years ago it was produced when China was ruled by Kuomintang. During its third performance KMT soldiers closed door and arrested many. Their clever detectives saw Don José's stabbing Carmen as war between Mao Zedong and Chiang Kaishek."

Then she got up from the table and walked over to the piano, offering Sissy her hand.

"Yes?" she smiled.

"Yes. In truth, I'd love to work with you," Sissy returned the smile and accepted her hand.

"And what about Sonny, what is his story?"

Rehearsal had ended early, and leaving the Tianqiao together, Xiaomei and Sissy decided to stop at a hotel near Tiananmen Square for something to drink.

"Well, he was his mother's oldest. He started piano when he was eleven, about the same time he started locking himself in the bathroom for hours at a time reading every word of every issue of *Reader's Digest* and *The New England Journal of Medicine* that his mother subscribed to. At sixteen he went to the Putney School up in Vermont, and later studied with Serkin at Marlboro College. Once on a bet he spent an entire weekend in lower Manhattan looking for Horowitz who was known to frequent those gay bars disguised as a Mr. Johnson. Now he's teaching at the ACM in Chicago, where we met six years ago right after I finished at Indiana and was doing a night-spot downtown."

"That was quick. Another cup?" Xiaomei asked, motioning to the waiter with the slight but unmistakable nod of the head of someone used to being obeyed.

"Yes," Sissy said, checking her watch. "Sonny won't be home for a couple more hours."

"And what about his family?"

"Ah, that's more difficult," Sissy paused. "It's very complicated, and it's still not at all clear."

"It is said that family stories in China are never clear," Xiaomei reached into her purse to pay the waiter.

"Well, as far as I can tell, that is, as far as Sonny can tell, his father was a psychologist and his mother a physician and he was born in Chongqing just before the end of the war. . . ."

". . . Sonny was born in China?" Xiaomei looked surprised.

"Oh yes, he moved with his parents to America when he was two and now travels on an American passport and pays his taxes. But it's not clear at all if his father was his father," Sissy paused, checking the details.

"I mean, Xiaomei," she continued, a bit more certain of her narrative, "he isn't sure that the man who acted in his father's place was really his father, and his mother has been deliberately vague when Sonny's pursued it. In fact, now they rarely talk or see each other."

Xiaomei listened, completely attentive, taking it all in.

"She's retired and lives in San Francisco, and still lectures her children whenever she gets a chance. Her live-in husband, he died nineteen years ago. But Sonny doesn't believe that his mother ever married his supposed father. Sonny suspects that his grandfather banished his real father," Sissy said and leaned forward a little, as if she and Xiaomei were unraveling a state secret. "And then perhaps they were the only ones left who knew each other as family in that tumultuous political and military and personal upheaval and chaos in China at the end of the war, that you must know better than me or Sonny."

Here Sissy paused, reflective.

"When did they leave China?"

"When did they leave China? Nineteen forty-six. His supposed-father left for the States and his friends in Cambridge just accepted that the woman and child with him were his wife and son."

"Something's missing here," Xiaomei interrupted.

"Yes, a lot, and a lot of it is pure conjecture. And I'm not sure Sonny would want this to be made public," Sissy added.

"Of course," Xiaomei promised. "But this is a very common Chinese story in the turmoil of this century."

"You see, I think Sonny suspects his supposed-father was really his grandfather, I don't know. He keeps this part all to himself. Sometimes I can tell he's very troubled by it and becomes very non-communicative. A couple of times I've seen him stop practicing and look away from the music at absolutely nothing at all, like I imagined he'd looked into his mother's eyes for some clues, for some answers he's entitled to. But she is determined not to let go of the invented lives, and that's why they don't speak to each other any more."

Sissy stopped again, then added, "At least my people took care of their stories."

"Does Sonny have any siblings?" Xiaomei motioned for the waiter again.

"Well, this part is complicated too. He has an older half-brother, but maybe he's really Sonny's uncle, a mathematician. I met him once, at his sister's wedding. Unsettled since the day he was born, I remember him saying, he'd first thought of becoming a political geographer in the third grade where he'd learned the rudiments of boundaries. He said he was fascinated by the economics of such a ruthless lottery, and I think he should have been a writer instead of a mathematician. He taught math at a college in Wisconsin, then quit altogether, and has settled his personal space between working for Westinghouse in Pittsburgh and consulting at Los Alamos, New Mexico, between truth and consequence, he said to me that afternoon, perhaps a little bit drunk, and added that there was no other truthful way to answer my question about himself."

"Sissy, this sounds like our Sichuan ghost opera," said Xiaomei, ordering Russian vodka for both of them.

"Sonny and his half-brother or half-uncle did not really get along with each other at home. Since the resident parents conspired to maintain their public stories at home too, the two boys did not have the language to understand their relationship to each other. So they kept this mutual distance, at least after Sonny's half-brother-uncle accidentally cut Sonny's left eyebrow, just missing his eye, there, you can still see the scar . . ."

"Yes, yes," Xiaomei pointed above her left eye.

". . . in a bamboo stick sword fight. At times Sonny has said that there had always been a curtain separating them, probably held up by his mother in her attempt to protect her own son and her attempt to protect the motherless half-brother-half-uncle too. In either case, she could do no right, her feet double-bound."

"And the father, what does Sonny say about him?"

"He stood by silent and benign, bitter, attentive to his hernia and strokes, worried over the McCarthyism, fighting off alcoholism and a disappearing dynamite career, writing his memoirs and preparing a book on the national character of China and, according to Sonny, funded by laundered grants from the CIA, the same source for Harold Cantrell's companion work on eastern Europe."

"And what about sister married in Cambridge?"

"She's younger than Sonny. It's clear enough who her father and mother were, since her brothers were old enough to remember the truth. So Sonny's sister grew up watching her siblings struggle with such a dilemma, sometimes from a distance, sometimes heartfelt near, and learned to be very practical. Now she has gone into business for herself, and lives in San Francisco with the same zip code as her mother, although they seldom see each other. Occasionally they would leave swallows' nest soup or kittens on each other's back porch or messages on each other's answering machine deliberately when they knew the other would be gone, carefully balanced between consent and forgiveness."

In the silence that followed, neither moved nor looked at the other.

"There's a novel here for someone," Sissy finally said, lightening the mood.

"Some story, Sissy. And then, then what else?"

"Sonny's been thinking recently that it's just possible that his mother and grandfather poisoned his half-brother-half-uncle's mother with white arsenic powder, that she could not have died of pneumonia, at least that was the public version as cause of death, not when there were three trained doctors in the house."

"Yes, very common for unwanted wives. But Sissy, how can you remember all this?" Xiaomei asked, her brows lifted at both the story and Sissy's breathless telling of it, as if she had not left a word out or changed a single word of it.

"It wasn't an effort, not when it's Sonny's personal story. We're very close. I was raised to be attentive to stories. I know Sonny's story as well as my own, and I've tried to tell his without changing anything."

"So why did Sonny come to Beijing?" Xiaomei finally asked.

"To get a feel for this country that might clarify his ambiguous background, he says. But I'm not so sure," Sissy said, looking down at her hands, not entirely convinced.

"Maybe for an explanation," she added. "Maybe to see how others have survived the same circumstances. Maybe for revenge. Maybe to lay blame. I don't know for sure."

More silence.

Finally Xiaomei said, "I know his story. It's still unfinished, our twentieth-century story, our grand opera. And you Sissy, why did you come to Beijing?"

"Oh, that's simple. I'm taking a vacation to be with him, see some of Beijing, and do Carmen."

Alex Kuo

Propped up in bed one evening a few days later, Xiaomei read the offprint of a 1972 *Journal of Comparative and Physiological Psychology* article about Sonny's father or grandfather which Sonny had given to Sissy to give to her.

"He said this'll explain his recital program," Sissy had told her, "whatever that means."

A radical environmentalist, Sonny's father was both rebellious and innovative. Politically he had been active with both Chiang Kaishek and Zhou Enlai, but during the turbulence of the war he could barely balance feeding the chickens he kept for his experiments and staying ahead of the Japanese, KMT and Communist armies. At the end of the war, at the height of his career at forty-eight, he left China again. But this time he did not return to it or to his work ever again, and instead wasted the rest of his life, Xiaomei concluded, the last twenty-four years working on his autobiography and a psychological analysis of the Chinese national character from Cambridge, Massachusetts.

And what happened to his chickens when he moved during the war, Xiaomei wondered. Did they simply just die of dehydration in the abandoned labs? Did he pass them off to the eager mouths of Chiang's mercenaries or Mao's insurgents? Or were the soldiers already on their way to his labs, for they had heard rumors that such casual flocks existed in some landlord's animal farm just waiting to be wrung, plucked and boiled, while he just packed up what he could carry ahead of them and slipped into the nearest exiting C-47 that gold could buy?

But the tragedy is the waste, she thought, the waste of the war and the revolution, of people killing people of infinite kin, or destroying their promising lives by exiling them into bitter impotence or the welcoming arms of the CIA or both. And now their children have returned to a country that had usurped their parents almost half a century ago. And for what? So Sonny had returned, returned to get a *feel* for the country of his parents, their background, and he was willing and daring enough to present himself in a most personal recital.

Xiaomei rushed out of bed to look at the printed program again: Schumann's *Kreisleriana,* Liszt's *Mazeppa Revenge,* Beethoven's Opus III. No intermission. Now for the first time, she understood the logic in Sonny's selections and their order, particularly the Liszt death-defying piece tucked in the middle, to throw in the face of the country that had killed both or all three of his parents, and to proclaim his personal statement of the triumph of individual will and talent not wasted.

Carefully centering the program on her piano's music stand, Xiaomei made up her mind that she was going to help him. She had been here before. And Sissy? She's a joy, she understands.

Five

SONNY HAD INSISTED that his student Liyuan have another lesson on the conservatory auditorium's nine-foot Steinway on which she'd be playing her master's degree recital in less than two days. He did not think her Chopin was ready, and had in fact thought of suggesting a last minute substitution, the Mozart D Minor Concerto she had played for another teacher last term, for which he would accompany her on an upright, getting rid of both the Chopin and Mozart's C Minor Fantasy altogether for the entire second half of her program. But he was stopped by the one certainty that had been consistently affirmed since his arrival in Beijing — changes of concept, habit or heart were near impossible.

"Stop. Stop. Go back and try that line again. And end it with the fourth or fifth finger this time, and lightly, your key attack is too quick, too much arm," Sonny interrupted Liyuan's Chopin from the back of the auditorium.

Liyuan stopped and glared at him, then picked up the music from the floor and opened it, squinting at her notes.

"But you said the second finger, here, you marked the score," she looked up and protested.

"It doesn't work, your second finger's too heavy. Just try it, try it with a lifting fourth."

Liyuan dropped her music and played through the same passage again, her frustration conflicting with her determination.

"That's it, that's it, that's much better," Sonny interrupted again. "Now try the whole section without hesitation. Make the thirds sound natural, don't accentuate them."

"But Chopin composed this as teaching aid, as technique demonstration," Liyuan was adamant this time.

"Oh, come off it. That may well be true Liyuan, but you're not a pupil anymore. When you're up there performing, you have to make music out of it. Otherwise take it off your program, if you're just going to demonstrate a technique."

One of Liyuan's inattentive fingers slipped onto a white key, its note's decaying sound reverberating around the auditorium before she killed it with the dampers. Then she raised both wrists, paused, and started at the beginning of the section.

"That's nice, that's nice," Sonny said above her playing. "Now legato, legato. Legato please, and connect those upper notes, no, no, not with the pedal, yes, that's it, good, good, excellent, bravo."

Liyuan got past the thirds, but sounded hesitant in the arpeggios that followed, demurring at the end of phrases, almost disappearing.

"Stop, stop, Liyuan. Listen, Chopin's got to be played straight up, the way it looks on the page. Don't rewrite it like the Europeans. Keep the time steady, regular. You can't take away in the acceleration and try to give it back at the end. This is not a revolution. What's lost is lost, you can't restore it, you've got to go on."

"But cassette you let me borrow? Beijing people like playing that way."

"That's only to listen to, to hear someone else's idea, not to copy. Horowitz is dead already. There's only Arrau and Michelangeli left. If we don't find another, the piano's dead."

"But you contradict. You say second, then third, then fourth. You say listen, then you say ignore it. You confuse me, teacher Ling," Liyuan lowered her head, and sounded almost ready to give up everything.

"Liyuan," Sonny got up and said slowly. "Liyuan, listen, I can't be your teacher and stand behind you for the rest of your life. You've got to learn to choose, you've got to make your own decisions. This may not sound very socialist, but as a musician you can't afford to just imitate, imitate, imitate.

You've got to commit to your own choices. That is the difference between a musician and a crowd-pleaser."

Liyuan looked at Sonny slowly, just slowly enough around all the hope and all the promise and all the talent, until a slight glimmer appeared in her eyes under the stage spotlights, diminishing her doubt. She threw her hair back, and with confidence restarted the Chopin from the very beginning.

"Lightly, lightly now. Lightly, lightly please," Sonny continued from the back of the auditorium. "Excellent, but don't be so dutiful, try a little invention."

Madame Zhou looked at Sonny in his jeans and white cotton shirt buttoned at the wrists and smiled.

Dressed in a formal gown of deep red silk brocade with high collar, Madame Zhou walked up to him backstage and gave him both her hands.

"You look wonderful, and you look ready," she said.

"Thank you," Sonny muttered, and accepted her kiss, unbuttoning his shirtsleeves and turning each back in two neat folds. "How's Xiaomei doing in the foyer?"

"I think she's just finished her lecture," Madame Zhou said, peering through the curtains. "She has been doing this for ten years, before she conducts Western opera. She has prepared them for your marathon. Here she is walking down the right aisle."

Sonny peered through the curtains, and saw Xiaomei in a navy blue silk suit sit down in the third row, between Sissy and a man who must be the American ambassador in a dark tuxedo.

"It seems to be a full house," he said, letting the curtains fall back.

"Yes, one thousand one hundred and thirty-seven exactly," Madame Zhou announced. "Every seat occupied."

Sonny looked across the stage into the glare of the houselights at the nine-foot Steinway which had been tuned yesterday morning and at his insistence again this afternoon by an androgynous-looking woman with very short hair. Sonny had been very happy with her work, and felt good that he had decided on the Steinway. The Bosendorfer was still too new, and the uppers sounded too thin and brittle to hold the last movement of the Beethoven. He'd also liked the ease of the Steinway action, which gave him the breathing space he needed for the Liszt, and its long decay time would help hold up the Schumann.

"Sonny?"

"I'm ready," he said, letting his arms drop and shaking them loose.

At a nod from Madame Zhou, the houselights were dimmed and the spot focused on the fully-opened Steinway.

Alex Kuo

Breathing deeply and steadily in this moment he had come to China for, Sonny walked out to the front of the stage and bowed as slightly as his smile to acknowledge the audience's polite but very hesitant applause. They had come to listen to an American pianist, *The People's Daily* had announced, and they had expected a white person in a tuxedo, Sonny later learned from Xiaomei.

Into the *Kreisleriana* now. Sonny concentrated on its patience, patience with the tremendous variety of possibilities, letting the lines sing as they were written, without improvisation — no soulful self-indulgence in nineteenth-century melancholia or turbulent schizophrenia here, but intelligence and graceful distance. There, the weight from the shoulder, *vivace assai,* suspension, breathing, breathing, the wrists leading. There will be a tomorrow, the sustained octave legato of the dotted rhythms ever so lightly, the percussive finger-work into the sixteenth notes in both hands now, and the final subtle rhythmic changes before tomorrow comes, unfrustrated by invention.

Keeping head down, fingers hovering over the keys, to keep the audience from applauding, then ready, steady, breathing in, go, go, *Mazeppa,* and Sonny graphically violent into the dark, in enemy territory now, into that mad catastrophic diaspora between war and revolution, returning in that colossal arpeggiated revenge, taking the notes to their boiling point marked *trionfante,* the diminished sevenths here holding everything all together, let it go, nail it, there.

But still head down, a little, little breathing, even before the chance for applause, a little detached here at the beginning, Sonny believed Beethoven knew it was going to be his last piano piece but still couldn't resist the contrasting statements. Into the middle now, the *cantabile* before the variations, let it sing, let it sing as slowly as possible without breaking apart.

And now the last, long variation, what Sonny had been waiting for all his life, lightly, ever so lightly everywhere now, into the point-blank triple trills where all the notes faced each other in equal velocity, subdued sharp and clear, into the *espressivo* short transition, let it out here but again without indulgence, the only place so marked in the entire piece, and just as quickly, seamless, back to that tranquility and unencumbered dignity, floating and distancing, lilting here in compensation in these final high semiquavers, celebrating that space in solitude, and without regret, rising into that final magnificent evaporation.

The American flag unfurled to the side of the hood, the ambassador's black Cadillac stretch-limousine with the black 0224-00001 diplomatic plates and smoked glass took them all to his residence for the reception after the recital. They passed other embassy compounds, and Sonny imagined that they could have been driving down Connecticut Avenue in DC or any other national capital on a late winter night. Except for a few errant cyclists, the sidearmed Beijing police sentries at the gates to these compounds were all the people that he could see between the Beijing Concert Hall and the US Embassy. It was close to ten o'clock at night in Beijing, and Madame Zhou had been right: they like to get home by nine here.

In his polyester green suit with white belt and matching white shoes, the ambassador congratulated Sonny again as the limousine pulled past the Marine guards at attention.

"That was marvelous, that was just really great," he said. "You've done justice to all the oriental Americans."

Before he could say anything, Sonny could feel Sissy's sharp elbow in his side. "Thanks, thanks for coming, and thanks for this reception," he said instead.

Sissy had been all smiles; she smiled at everyone and no one during the entire reception, and so did her friend Xiaomei who for once was speechless, and Madame Zhou as well.

"I'll tell you exactly how good you were later," Sissy whispered to him in the only brief moment they were alone together in the huge living room, smiling at everybody else.

After Xiaomei joined them, Sonny said aloud that he suspected half of the embassy was filled with those Georgetown law graduates from Grand Rapids, Michigan, who couldn't even find an assistant's job in a DA's office, but found a home as career foreign service administrators in the State Department.

"Hush Sonny," Sissy said, still smiling. "They'll hear you, in a cave, all furry and growling."

"I'm sorry that I wasn't able to attend your concert tonight," a man with a diminishing Bronx-accent said to Sonny. "But we heard that you were great."

"Thanks, thanks. That's quite a set-up you've got here." Sonny took a sip of his vodka and asked, "Where're you from?"

"Oh, Michigan."

"Where in Michigan?" Sonny pressed.

"Oh, a small town, Grand Rapids."

"Oh yeah, Gerald Ford's turf. Where'd you go to school?"

"Oh," he hesitated, then added, "Georgetown law."

"Oh, I'm sorry," Sonny said. "I mean I'm sorry that you couldn't make it to the recital tonight."

"Sonny, Sonny Ling," Xiaomei approached him, followed by a man who looked decidedly like he did not want to be there inside the American ambassador's residence.

"Sonny, I want to introduce you to Cao Feng. He reviews music for the Xinhua publications. Mr. Cao, this is Mr. Ling."

"You were tremendous tonight," Cao greeted Sonny, extending his hand. "Incredible music."

"Thanks," Sonny murmured, never a person able to accept congratulations graciously or easily.

"It was amazing, how the audience accepted the two-hour recital. Not a single person left at nine. In the last section of the Beethoven, I saw some of the older persons crying. You were very convincing."

"What a generous review," said Sissy, who'd just joined them.

"You believed in the music you were playing, a breathless conviction, and we did too. The audience wanted an encore," Cao said.

"I had planned on doing Variations 25, 26 and 30 of the *Goldberg*, but it didn't feel right. I've spent my life avoiding doing the expected, like banging out Rach 3 on five continents. Not even Madame Zhou could talk me into it."

"I think I understand," Cao replied. "Yes, I think there was more than just music tonight in your playing."

"Mr. Cao," Xiaomei interrupted. "I agree. I think Sonny made a statement tonight."

"*Shenme?*"

"I think Mr. Ling said something defiant and assertive and hopeful to us tonight," she clarified.

"And such superb music," added Madame Zhou, who had just joined this gathering segregated to the side of the American ambassador's living room in Beijing.

Six

FROM THE EMBASSY RECEPTION Cao Feng walked straight to his shared desk at the Xinhua office at Xuanwumennei Xi. Even though he had compiled copious notes during Sonny's recital, he had wanted to write its review while his memory of the startling performance was still vivid.

The American pianist Sonny Ling, Cao Feng started his review on the computer, but he stopped and thought about the name *Sonny Ling*. Before Feng dropped out of law school, he had taken a writing course named "Evidence" taught by the upstart writer Wang Meng, who had said in a lecture that writing is a form of combustion. This stayed with Feng and eventually inspired his defection to journalism.

Recently Feng had been writing short stories secretly on the Xinhua computer, being ever so meticulous in erasing everything before he left his desk and carefully tucking the printouts into his inside coat pocket. Ever since Zheng Xiaomei had confirmed his suspicions that there had been something very political about Ling's recital, Cao Feng had wanted to write a story about him, and not just a review of his performance.

It was the same when last month he had heard a rumor about a woman who had tried to jump from a thirteenth-floor window of the tall Bank of China building at Fuchengmennei. When he interviewed the bank officials for a newspaper story, he was politely referred to the Ministry of Public Security, and there, even with his Xinhua official government news agency press credentials, he was referred to the Beijing Bureau of Public Security, then to the Beijing Fire Department, the Beijing Statistical Bureau, the Bureau of Religious Affairs.

Finally, after a week of doggedly pursuing each and every lead, an old journalist's habit he had not discarded, he was sent back to the Bank of China where he had started. In the end, he had decided to go ahead and write the story from his imagination, which he thought would be more truthful anyway. He had entitled the story *Smoke*.

SMOKE

Shen Zang was walking to his office when he was picked up by two Public Security agents and rushed across town in an unmarked car. Police and fire trucks had already surrounded the main Bank of China building on Fuchengmennei when he arrived, the gathering crowd looking up at the woman barely hanging by her fingers on the ledge of the thirteenth floor.

"How long has she been there?" Shen asked.

"We don't know for sure. Some have said two hours, others, all her life, and that person over there," the captain with the double red braids on his epaulets said, shaking his walkie-talkie's rubber antenna in the direction of a tall and dark-skinned woman with a music case, "she said four thousand years."

These answers had become more ambiguous since Shen became the first head of the recently established State Bureau of Psychology. Within two days of the announcement of his appointment being released by the Xinhua News Agency to the press and television, along with his photograph, strangers started to stop him in the streets with their detailed life stories, some offering reasons to live, others he wasn't so sure about. As the director of this national repository of mental health in a modernizing nation, he had to accept these offers of advice, even when he could not distinguish rumor from lore, or report from minimalism.

Last week he had to confront the case of a man who had threatened to drown himself in two inches of basin water, and mediate between the Premier and his wife who was threatening to leave him for Henry Kissinger after attending an Elton John concert at the Tianqiao. In fact, since appointed, he had yet to appear in his office, and had yet to learn the size, exact function and names of his staff, and the linkages with the other ministries, bureaux and emergency and public security units, a process that would surely require a year of phone calls and meetings.

"Do you have a net?" Shen asked the police captain.

"A net? Why, if she wants to jump, she jumps."

"But my job is to stop her."

"That's not mine. I'm here for crowd control, and to investigate how someone could have passed through Bank of China security. Maybe the fire captain has a net."

Shen could sense that the onlookers were beginning to get anxious, that something tragic was about to happen. From his American psychiatric training, which specialized in coincidental meanings, he had learned to tell when everything will happen as intended and at the right time, and when it won't. This was a *won't,* unless something intervened quickly.

The fire captain had already radioed for a net, but at this moment he was busily coordinating a surgical extraction operation between the PLA's rapelling crew waiting on the fourteenth floor, and the police's anti-student-terrorist squad on the twelfth. So Shen took the express elevator on the left up to the thirteenth, and cautiously approached the opened window.

"Don't come any closer," the woman said.

Shen assured her that he wouldn't, that he just wanted to talk with her, that he had a story which she must listen to if she had hung on to life for so long.

"Don't you even want to hear why I'm up here trying to end my life?"

"Yes, of course, but will you let me help you climb back up if I listen?"

There was no answer, but in her silence Shen began to describe to her the group of one hundred women dressed in black who have gathered every day for three years in Jerusalem, a silent protest against oppression. Every day rightists and leftists by jeep-loads encircle them, spitting at them, but they say nothing, and return again the next day. They have done this for centuries, most recently in Buenos Aires and Greenham Common, these mothers who look after our promises.

"Ask yourself this," Shen said at the end of the story. "Ask yourself what kind of promises they have made to each other, and what kind of promise you have made to yourself."

There was a slight sigh, as if the wind had carried it up from the dark-skinned woman with the music case thirteen floors below.

"If I did, will you trade places with me?" the woman at the window finally asked.

Shen looked down at the uplifted faces thirteen floors down, at all the fire trucks and police vans, and then at the woman's whitened fingers clinging onto the edge, all of them imperfect heartbeats in the middle of the current.

So at one in the morning at his shared desk at the Xinhua, Feng started jotting down notes for the story based on Sonny Ling that he wanted to write. He had decided that in order to replicate the recital as much as language would permit, he would have to find a metaphor that would hold up under several levels of interpretation and translation. But that search could wait; right now he just wanted to concentrate on the meaning of Zheng Xiaomei's words for describing the recital, *made a statement tonight,* and *defiant, assertive and hopeful.* Feng remembered that when Zheng used her conductor's deliberate intonation to underscore her intended meaning, these words seemed to have lost their neutrality and leaned toward the political. He had to be very careful here, he reminded himself. Any slip in attention to the evidence however inconsequential now would diminish his critical capacity for finding what they signified. What if his informant was wrong, what if Zheng Xiaomei had completely misinterpreted Sonny Ling's recital, or what if she had purposely misled him, and for what express purpose?

He had not felt right about being in the American Embassy either, particularly when the group gathered around Ling, the guest of honor at the reception, was comprised only of Chinese. Where was the host, or anyone else in that white diplomatic corps? He had dismissed it at the time, thinking that the group had been defined by their interest and involvement in music and not race, but he was not so sure now.

Feng could find no answer that was in itself satisfactory. He was stuck, so he filled his pen, leaned back in his chair and looked out the window at the lights from the Broadcasting Building and thought about pursuing the rumors he had been hearing all week, that some university students in the Haidian District, prompted by a Tsinghua physics professor's concern with government corruption, had been overheard planning a demonstration at Tiananmen Square. Suddenly two words focused in his mind, and he jotted them down on the corner of a small piece of paper on his desk, *point* and *blank,* and slipped it into his coat pocket.

In the meantime, he made himself write out the Ling recital review:

Last night Beijing concert-goers were treated to a sensational piano recital at the Beijing Concert Hall by the American Chinese virtuoso Sonny Ling.

Before he started playing to a full house, our famous director Zheng Xiaomei greeted the audience inside the foyer and explained the complicated and difficult program of Schumann's *Kreisleriana,* Liszt's *Mazeppa Revenge* Study, and Beethoven's last piano sonata, Opus III.

What she did not mention was that Mr. Ling would not take an intermission; indeed, he did not permit any applause until the entire program was over.

An extraordinary musician, Mr. Ling's convincing renditions made a statement tonight, asserting both his exceptional talent and his defiance of the traditional interpretations of these complex pieces.

In the end, the standing ovation was deafening, even after this unusually long recital for our Beijing audience. The absence of any encore only reinforced Mr. Ling's individual voice.

Two days later, back at his desk, Feng was convinced that the title to his story should be *Point Blank,* even though he was still not definite about the story he expected it to carry. He knew that he did not want to just duplicate what everyone else was writing, those neo-realistic novels that were still trying to deal with China's national wound from the Cultural Revolution, the first revolution in human history in which one did not have to believe in anything. In fact, he did not even think that it was an issue anymore. But the critics and publishers liked them because the novels conformed to the linear development of the socialist narrative, even though one of the publishers openly admitted that the often-subsidized first printing rarely exceeded four thousand in a nation of over one billion.

Feng wanted his novel to reflect what the revolution really meant today, exactly forty years after Mao declared its success atop Tiananmen in 1949. Mao had triumphed over random individual acts of will. For centuries people had witnessed acts of unbelievable acrobatics, levee construction and tiger-killing, after which the fleeced audience went home from this bazaar exhausted and satisfied that the universe had once more been confronted and conquered, the kingdom secured for personal domesticity, except for those few children who dared to be different. These children are still out there in the twilight or at night in the June-bug light practicing for that next encounter, balancing or juggling or twirling or sighting along a rifle barrel, or fasting, ready at any moment to assume for the community the role of its hero or martyr, or sucker, or defeated lunatic. Feng wanted to ask how, after the triumph of ideology over anarchy and despotism, the national passion for revolution ever got maneuvered into a passion for washing machines or blusher.

He also wanted the novel to ask whether it was true that what the revolution really gave the people was not individual dignity and economic promise, but the right to be stupid as well as the right to be consequently arrogant. He thought that only fiction could understand and explain how a revolution could culminate in a nation that colonized itself, unfit for death, day by day little wisps of hope evaporating into instant lies four hundred times every day, and feigned exaggerations in the burgeoning bureaucracy. If the truth be discovered, as he'd suspected it would be, within such a context, then ideology has no compelling urgency, (that's why he had left law twenty-five years ago), and language merely functioned as aphorisms in which a white horse can be anything one wanted it to be at any given moment, Mao or no Mao.

In this way he found the opening sentence: "When the exiled son of China's last revolution that tried to end feudalism, bourgeois capitalism and imperialism but instead arrested everyone's hope, returned to his homeland half a century later, he demanded some answers to this sacrifice for which his parents had already paid the price."

But Feng had an uneasy feeling about this line. It sounded too much like a plot summary for one of those Chinese revenge operas with heroic Shakespearean characteristics, hah hah, which Mao's wife Jiang Qing saw as being so feudal and against the spirit of social equality that she successfully banned them from being performed during the Cultural Revolution. He also suspected the truth of such a narrative after developing some serious doubts about the success of Mao's revolution, when he started thinking of the history of China as a centuries-long obscene civil war in which the enemy could be anyone: brother, mother, friend, or since 1949, the government as well, hah hah.

Lately he had also started feeling uncomfortable about certain things happening around him this spring, ever since his attempt to track down the story of the window leaper. He had started collecting small, found things, some coins, paper clips, little pieces of stones found on the sidewalk, and storing them in his overcoat pockets.

Seven

At FIVE IN THE MORNING of the day of *Carmen,* Sissy was up early making coffee and singing softly to herself in the bathroom from Astrud Gilberto's *Forgive Me* cassette she had brought with her to Beijing. But it was just enough to wake up Sonny, as her singing always had, as if his inner ear was tuned to her voice. Sissy, on the other hand, could sleep through Sonny's practices at home, even without a drop-curtain in the piano.

By the time Sonny padded to the opened door of the bathroom in the slippers that were too small for him, Sissy had the fingers of one hand pressed to her throat and was watching herself in the mirror hum her gypsy song from the opening of Act II.

"Oh, did I wake you up," she stopped humming and talked to Sonny in the mirror. "I'm sorry."

"Hi. You're getting an early start. Don't use it all up now, you've got fourteen hours to go."

"Oh yeah," she said and turned around, smiling, reaching out to Sonny. "And just what d'you suggest we do in all that time?"

Sonny took her hands and then kissed her lips and pressed her against the sink.

"Good morning," he whispered.

"Good morning. You know Sonny, I've been thinking," Sissy said, smiling. "D'you think Carmen's a slut?"

"No, just someone who wanted a life for herself," Sonny answered, pulling back a little.

"Yes. Yes, you're right. But have you ever thought of the story?"

"What d'you mean?" Sonny said, reaching for his toothbrush.

"I mean, maybe Bizet got it all wrong, I mean," Sissy got out the toothpaste. "Maybe he and that French writer Merimée got it all wrong. Wrong country. This is not a Spanish story, it's a Chinese story, and that's why *Carmen* is so popular here."

"And then," Sissy continued, rinsing her mouth, "and then, what do you think happened to Don José?"

"You mean after he kills Carmen?"

"Yah. Is he going to be punished?"

"I don't think so. As a dragoon he was keeping the peace which Carmen was threatening."

"Hm, you think so? You think it's all that simple?" Sissy mocked, beginning a step that would land them both back in bed. "And I suppose you think that Escamillo is a hero?"

"Yeah, a regular Mao."

She did not fuss over this comparison, but instead helped Sonny with her own shirt buttons, while reaching down around his buttocks with her other hand. Free now, she thought, free now. She felt the recognition between their bodies, and knew that she would remember this morning years from now, too, there, there, the tip of it waiting in sweet linen, slow desperado riding the waves of seeping morning light.

"Oh Sonny, there, bite me there, oh shit," she whispered.

"They want another curtain call," the prompter with the short hair said to Xiaomei, Sissy and Don José's Xue Shi, who were standing together offstage and beaming at each other, their arms filled with iris, forget-me-not and rose bouquets.

". . . and your dancing, fantastic," Xue Shi complimented Sissy.

"Thanks, and you were great yourself. You didn't even change your tempo when I accidentally bumped into your knife in the fight scene."

"Yes, I saw from the orchestra pit and worried for a moment," Xiaomei said. "But you were so good, you sang and danced like a woman who could not be stopped, just like *Carmen*. Here Sissy," she offered her a handkerchief that was tucked into her sleeve, "your eye makeup is running, those hot spotlights."

"Please, conductor Zheng," the prompter asked again. "They want you out there, another bow."

Xiaomei gave her baton to the prompter and reached once more for Sissy's and Xue Shi's hands, the three of them walking out into the thunderous standing ovation.

When they were back moments later, the applause had not diminished.

"Why hasn't the curtain closed?" Xiaomei asked a stagehand.

"It's stuck, conductor Zheng," he said sheepishly.

For the first time since Sissy had known her, even through some very difficult rehearsals coordinating the dancers, chorus and orchestra, Xiaomei looked a little disturbed.

"Oh no, you don't mean the applause'll go on forever?" Sissy asked.

"Hah, hah, it might. In China one never knows what will happen next."

The voice had come from a gentlemen approaching Sissy from the wing. Sissy turned and recognized him at once from the airport.

"Professor Luo!" Sissy threw out her arms.

"Yes, but you must go out again," he said, pushing her away and clapping his hands. "The applause is for you."

"Yes, go Sissy," Xiaomei joined Professor Luo.

Out under the spotlight Sissy felt the burgeoning applause that would not stop. Deeply moved, she reached into her bouquet for the roses and tossed them into the front rows, one by one, as Carmen would have done.

When she thought it was finally polite to return to back-stage, Professor Luo and Xiaomei and Xue Shi were still applauding.

"Professor Luo," Sissy continued beaming. "How nice of you to come."

"I saw your name in newspaper."

"Oh yes," Sissy looked in her excitement to Xiaomei, who had just asked the house manager to dim the stage lights. "Xiaomei, this is Professor Luo, the man who was so helpful to me at the airport. This is conductor Zheng Xiaomei, my friend."

The two of them shook hands. It was getting exceptionally crowded and loud backstage. The singers, dancers and music-ians were joyfully congratulating each other and Sissy and Xiaomei and Xue Shi. They could barely hear what any one else was saying.

Sonny struggled his way through the crowd and brought Sissy one single rose and a tight hug.

"You were absolutely great, just great," he beamed, "even when you took their chances."

"Thanks, thanks, Sonny. Sonny, this is Professor Luo, the mathematician returned from Australia I told you about. Professor, this is Sonny, my friend."

"But, but you look like Chinese," Luo said, looking a little startled. "I thought you American."

"Well yes, both my parents were Chinese, if that's what you mean," Sonny shook his hand.

"You Americans confuse me."

"We confuse ourselves sometimes," Sissy responded.

"And Sissy, your singing was so fine. I did not know you knew French?"

"I don't, but singing is different. I think it's easier to learn a language singing it than speaking it."

"I enjoyed your singing tonight; I think I understood. My first Western opera," Luo continued. "I never understood Western music, just Chinese opera, and that was criticized as feudal when I was in school, except for official-approved eight. Maybe I come again now, director Zheng?"

When Professor Luo Zhiquan arrived at his graduate seminar on finite numbers at Tsinghua University the next morning, most of his best students in the class were absent. He knew where they had gone to, and he wanted to ask these other remaining students, *Why aren't you with the rest of your class-mates?* He had heard many descriptions of recent events at Tiananmen Square, and discovered for the first time how he felt about his country's fascist government, albeit in the second-person. He spent the last several evenings thinking about the issues that the students had raised and trying to define his personal responsibility to them. By the time he remembered that he had left Canberra to return to China because he had not been very happy giving his abstract lectures to an Australian audience — which had not particularly made him feel welcomed but more like a legal alien, needed but unwanted — the answer had become alarmingly clear. He decided he would not be quiet and invisible in his own country, especially not now when so many others more vulnerable than him were beginning to speak up.

"Where are your friends?" Zhiquan asked the class, carefully looking at their faces.

No one said anything, and no one looked at him or at each other. Finally the student from Changchun, the one with the highest grades although Zhiquan suspected that he didn't know much of anything at all, rose to his feet.

"They are boycotting this class and have gone to Tiananmen Square to stir up trouble and instigate more illegal turmoil," he announced in a loud voice, slapping his desk for emphasis.

Another student, one of the only two women in the class, also stood up, turned and faced him.

"That is not true. They went to Tiananmen to present a petition to Premier Li Peng at the Great Hall of the People. They are asking him to stop government corruption."

Zhiquan sensed that he had to be very careful dealing with this micro version of what was happening outside the classroom — he was optimistic enough to want everyone in the class to learn something from this experience, however benign or dangerous it might be.

"Please sit down," he said. "And you do not have to shout in my classroom," he added.

He waited until the two students had sat down before continuing.

"There are tumultuous events happening outside our class this week. Historically this has happened to Beijing before — exactly seven times this century Beijing has witnessed and participated in and initiated those tremendous national changes resulting from such protest, dissidence and demonstration. Count them, starting with the Boxers: 1900, 1912, 1919, 1927, 1949, 1966. And the one most recently: 1976."

He wrote these numbers on the chalkboard, then turned to look at each student in turn.

"In one way or another," he continued, "Beijing's students have been central participants in these events, and in at least three of them have provided impetus and leadership."

Zhiquan waited a moment. His students were quiet, absorbed and anxious for him to continue, all but that top student from Changchun, who was busily taking down notes.

"Tsinghua University has been praised as China's MIT. But we have also been criticized as being unpatriotic and non-political. Tucked away in the outskirts of western Beijing Haidian District, some say because we are scientists we have been more victims of social and political change than those peasants who tend the rice fields and vegetable patches which still surround our campus. They say we do not think. They say we are happy just to take orders, whether they come from emperors, Dr. Sun, Kuomintang, Mao Zedong, Jiang Qing, Red Guards, Deng Xiaoping, or Party Central Committee. And in many ways they have been correct."

He looked around the seminar room again. His students appeared to be more attentive to this lecture than to his previous discussions of the properties and functions of finite numbers. Even the student from Changchun had put down his pencil and was beginning to look up.

"Perhaps history is being transformed again. Do you want to be one to tell your grandchildren that during this transformation which shaped your generation and brought China into twenty-first century, you were just squatting in middle of rice paddy outside Beijing satisfied counting numbers and dreaming of better job and more money? Go out there, see how change is being made. Go out there now and see what change is being made. It cannot hurt you to know. Class dismissed."

On his way to his bicycle to go to Tiananmen Square, Zhiquan thought about the possible consequences of his lecture and dismissal of class. Personally he was ready to accept whatever they might be. He had been here before and had paid the price for doing nothing — banished from his home, family and job to toil away in the barely arable fields two thousand *li* away for three years. He had now at least chosen the reason, if he was to be punished again.

Living by himself in a foreign country in semi-exile, he had been forced into scrutinizing his homeland, and had consequently struggled with the meaning of home, and for the first time in his life seemed to have understood it. He had not chosen to leave Australia and return to China because his life in Canberra was all demeaning and inconsequential; he had come back to give himself another chance to fully live the life of a citizen in his own home: defection, however justified, seldom worked politically or personally — he did not want to spend the rest of his life plotting revenge and memorizing another constitution in a foreign language.

Chinese Opera

Zhiquan listened to a speech given by a white-shirted student who had climbed onto the Monument to the People's Heroes and was holding a bullhorn in one hand and waving a petition in his other. Tiananmen Square was absolutely jammed, packed with students, workers and the law, like a carnival, but it had a grotesque edge to it, as if at any moment the whole scene could break apart. Swaying patriotic-red banners with large characters dotted the square, almost obliterating the Beijing skyline. Several speeches were being given simultaneously from each one of the monuments. Zhiquan thought that some of the police were listening as attentively as the students and workers.

"We are not cowards," the student said through the bullhorn. "We are not a nation of cowards. We have stood up against feudalism and imperialism many times before and we can do it again. When we fought the Japanese, we were fighting for our own rights. Now we must fight for our own rights again. We must oppose dictatorship that takes away our rights. We must topple the one-party system that chokes us. We must oppose leadership that has molded its citizens to thrive on commodity gratification. The moment is now. What are we waiting for? What are we waiting for? Another cataclysmic earthquake?"

These speeches were beginning to sound alike, Zhiquan thought, the issues deflected to slogans, metaphors and homilies. While basically valid arguments were presented, they were oversimplified, perhaps a necessity reflecting the traditional symbiotic dynamics between the students and the rest of the country. Zhiquan was also troubled by a couple of students whose speeches reflected a grotesque obsession with becoming bloody martyrs.

But perhaps the students had a point, as did the Red Guards too, although they went about it in the wrong, though only way, that ultimately demolished its own purpose and everything else that stood in its way. Perhaps the students were attempting to close the distance between the intellectuals and the workers again, for the eighth time this century.

Zhiquan was familiar with those Tsinghua professors who were only involved in activities that promoted their own personal careers and fame, a functional, self-centered literacy that was allowed them, but denied the critical and social literacy to criticize and thus to transform the world into a better place. They turned their heads while the politicians of the country, mostly uneducated beyond the eighth-grade, were exercising absolute freedom in ordering the country into whatever served their own personal interests best. Zhiquan thought that the student should have said, *We are not cowards; the intellectuals are the cowards,* but they asked instead, *Are we living a life in which a good death is worse than a bad life?*

Back at his Tsinghua office, Zhiquan wanted to take some of the heat off the students by writing a letter to *The People's Daily* supporting their position.

On the long bicycle ride back in this long Beijing spring, he had thought the letter would introduce some other issues as well as propose some specific solutions to those raised by the speeches he had heard at Tiananmen Square. He would begin by acknowledging the miracles of China practically eliminating hunger and homelessness in just forty years. But he wanted the country to go on. He wanted to see an end to mistaking privilege for talent. He wanted to see the constitution dismantled, because in its present form, amendments would have to originate with the party's Central Committee, thereby making the National People's Congress a white elephant of democratic rule; he wanted to see the money the country annually wasted on banquets, where nothing was traded but personal dignity, be channeled into education, housing and health care.

He wanted someone to rise up and invent a competing and compelling ideology so that the country would no longer feed on Mao or socialist-communism the same way some people sucked on religion or whiskey. He especially wanted the real China to stand up before the twenty-first century.

In short, he wanted to see the end to waste, fraud and the absence of dreams, the exact same things as the students.

But before he could start writing the letter, Zhiquan heard three light knocks on his office door.

Eight

WHEN SISSY ANSWERED the light knocking on her door, she was astonished to see the behind of a man in dark trousers bent over the top banister to see if anyone was following him.

"Zhiquan, what are you doing here?" she asked after he had turned around. "I hope you weren't waiting long, I had the TV on."

"*Ni hao,* Sissy. Is Sonny here?" Zhiquan asked, edgy and looking past Sissy into the apartment.

"What are you doing here?" Sissy asked again, waving Zhiquan into the apartment. "Your picture was on CCTV, at least it looked like you, I was so surprised. I didn't know what it meant, but it didn't sound good."

"Yes, yes, very bad, very bad, Sonny not here," Zhiquan took a step into the living room, but turned around to look behind him at the stairs. "I must go now."

"What's going on?" Sissy insisted.

"My student told me they are looking for me."

"What? What's going on?"

"Her father is high party member, he knows. She also said PLA killing people near Tiananmen Square."

"No. But why? And why are they looking for you?" Sissy asked slowly, beginning to anticipate the answers.

"I talked too much in class this morning," Zhiquan explained. "Now I must hide."

In the apartment's diminishing light of afternoon, a picture of Zhiquan appeared on the TV. Zhiquan walked over and turned up the sound.

". . . he is wanted for stirring up chaos and social unrest . . . threatening the country's stability. . . ."

"They are shooting people," Zhiquan said, after turning off the TV. "Many, many," he added, pointing towards downtown.

The noise of sirens could be heard now, one screaming by outside, replaced by its constant whine in the distance. They just stood there in the silence of the apartment, Sissy looking steadily over Zhiquan's shoulder and out the window, her eyes traveling further, mile after mile and generation before generation.

"This is like Sand Creek. This is Wounded Knee," Sissy finally said.

"*Shenme* Sissy? I must go now," Zhiquan started fidgeting and looking towards the door again. "I must disappear."

Sissy looked carefully at Zhiquan, her arm reaching out towards him and taking one of his hands.

"I can help you," she explained. "My people have been doing this for many generations. I can help you disappear; no one will find you."

When Sonny got back to the apartment, he found the door unlocked. Thinking that Sissy had just gone out for a moment, he lay down on the bed and was immediately swept into a deep sleep and ever deeper dream.

In this dream Sonny slowly riffled through the thick sheets of a picture album a second time, craning his neck over the colored images for a closer look. Each photograph shifted just a little, but enough to blur his most rudimentary visual distinctions in life: eyeglasses became mountain peaks; a ship's prow merged with the tail plumage of a Quetzal; his father into his son; his son-father, himself; man, woman. As his eyes got used to this way of looking at life, everything became everything else against an expanding kaleidoscope of colors.

He sat back and left the album open on an 8 x 10 enlargement of a high mountain lake, took his shoes and socks off and tucked them safely out of the way under his desk. The ducks and the dogs were already in the water when Sonny slipped himself in for the long swim across the deep-edged immensity. After his strokes and breathing became effortless and regular and he knew it was then possible, he began to exist, and he knew it. He wanted to believe that the birds and plants had left their taxonomic graveyards, that the animals had ceased being victims of tireless human cruelty and had gathered now in such extravagant murmuration. But another part of Sonny knew better — this could not be true, realism cannot be usurped, history is history. So he focused his attention instead on the topographical legends of the approaching opposite shore, its beach shimmering in the glare of the noonday sun.

Leaving the short drop of beach behind him, Sonny walked onto the parapets of a citrus county, its fruit furiously clapping with immense answers. On the next terrace in front of a shelter, the caretaker couple, runaways from the Guatemalan highlands, were answering some questions of travel asked by another, more recent defector, a Tiananmen Square main-lander. Together they accepted some food and something to drink offered in any language, shaded in the hint of a banyan tree from Sonny's distant childhood, lingering, marveling at the spread of sky, at the shifting wind in their lives, and at the color of the dissenting nationalist.

From this origin of hyphens, they wove their stories unhurriedly, an occasional *aaa-eh* acknowledging their intricate extensions, because they knew they were true even if it had not happened to them, even if it had no ending. Now and then a few ducks drifted in between their elaborations and settled at the crumbs by their side, their feet free of market ties. By then a light wind blew the thousand paper cranes in from Hiroshima, and what it brought reminded them to renew their determination.

Sonny stood up to leave, but as he took a last look at the Guatemalan couple and the Beijing intellectual whom he was just beginning to recognize, he knew he was them, there by the side of the shelter, and they were him, in this orchard, here now swimming strong, back across the lake there in that color photograph here together with the ducks and the dogs, in this picture that is every picture ever and no picture at all. A picture that he no longer needed because this will become memory that would keep and not shift and change, that this will be hope looking for a random child to give itself to, like that one waiting at the West Bank, rock already in hand, wishing that he understood more about the dust of stones and shifting strata beneath the ground on which he stood in his socks and his shoes.

"Sonny, Sonny, wake up," Sissy said, lightly kissing Sonny's lips.

"Huh, Sissy? Sissy? I've been dreaming," Sonny sat up. "You're back?

"Yes, I am back," Sissy sat down beside Sonny.

"What? You sound like you've been gone a long time," Sonny said, and then looked at the bedside clock. "What time is it?"

And before Sissy could answer, he continued.

"Sissy, listen, your Tsinghua friend, they're after him. His picture's all over CCTV. And they've started shooting already."

"Yes, I know, I know all of that."

She paused, and looked straight at Sonny before continuing.

"I helped him disappear. He's all right. I gave him my stories. . . ."

This is a house, and it does not have a door. In its place, choose an empty space, whether square, rectangle or circle, or any shape of your imagining, and walk through it with scruples. Our history is a history of doors and passages, of light to dark, or dark to light, or those journeys in between. But there is no door to this house, and we have already passed through what is not there.

Chinese Opera

In the diminishing light a student has picked up a rock. He hefts its weight in his hand and, taking careful aim at a tank the color of dirt, he heaves it. It strikes the turret mount with a hollow metallic sound as if no one was inside and bounces back into the street. Cameras from near and far record this moment. Is this why we have walked through the space of that house without a door, to see this and record it too? That student might well disappear later, depending on how far we've come, and give us an ending, a void in our hearts signifying his time and his place forever; and if we've come far enough, or not nearly far enough, his mothers would then collect his promises and gather in front of the ministry in silent vigil.

But we are too far of ourselves, as reliable as the metaphors seem to be. So let's step aside and check our omissions and exaggerations. There, the sun is rising unstoppable, nothing turning it back there. There are walls here too, some covered with revolutionary words, THE BIRD STILL LIVES in several colors. The only sound rising from the thronging crowd is an inept gasp anticipating irreversible dreams. We must move cautiously here, renew our identities, cross our hearts, if we are to avoid the stray lunatic endangering every species.

Then, there is that ten-year-old girl whose parents have left her to the side of her life, or she has left them, there's no escaping it, it's all the same in this kind of accident. There is also that mathematician who needs to be kept from the cruel politicians. They are both taking a pause here too, standing before Bogota or Beijing while across the street history is defining its martial laws.

With some spaces still empty in our passports, there is no reason why we can't take them with us. The little girl shrugs and they both ask, *Will there be sound of gunfire where we go?* The dreams are thickest here where there is no room for error. Even the promises that have stayed around long enough not to be noticed, are beginning to fluctuate. They are saying, *Look here, Look here,* in as many voices waiting to be counted. There are no explanations, and most of the time we don't even hear them, not even their symptoms, being what they are.

Look, the sky is beginning to close, we must go before the curfew descends on us. Remember, remember, the house we return to is the same one without the door. By now we must know exactly which one it is because we have never seen it before. Come, you too, we do not lie here, not even secretly. Goodbye, goodbye.

For the last two days Cao Feng had been hearing reports about Beijing's intellectuals harboring sympathy for their students' activism against government corruption, bureaucracy and nepotism. He had also heard that the Ministry of Public

Security was beginning to identify and arrest those known to have challenged Zhongnanhai's authority, especially in public. He was particularly drawn to rumors that some of these dissidents had disappeared beyond the police's elastic surveillance network.

Feng returned to his shared desk at the Xinhua, hoping to find some evidence that would help him distinguish wish from dream, dream from lore, and lore from lies. Absentmindedly thumbing through some sheaves of papers on his desk, he came across a rejected press dispatch, the bold cancellation stamp's red ink smudged by several fingertips. He read it, shielding his eyes from the naked light bulb in front of him.

A Beijing Public Security Bureau spokesman yesterday reportedly blamed lawless elements for spreading dissent and chaos that is beginning to threaten the stability of the nation.

Those intellectuals in Beijing's western suburbs engaged in fomenting these subversive activities were being investigated. Many arrests have been made. Some of these intellectuals' photographs have appeared on CCTV. Citizens have been asked to report their whereabouts to the nearest PSB office.

It has also been reported that a foreigner disguised as a Uygur or Tibetan compatriot has been seen helping some mathematics or physics professor from Tsinghua University disappear before the PSB could locate him.

The US Embassy has categorically denied that it has provided sanctuary for him, but the Ambassador was unavailable for comment.

Eyewitnesses provided conflicting reports of the disappearance. Some Beijingers swore that the foreigner was a woman who looked exactly like them. Others thought she was a tall Muslim from the north. Some were sure they had seen her at the Bank of China's main branch on Fuchengmennei, while others placed her as a saxophone player at the Shangri-La.

They all agreed that they were not certain about what they had witnessed, as if the images might have been a mirage. They also could not tell the direction of the couple's travel. "They just appeared, and then disappeared," one was heard to have said.

Feng read the story once more. Noticing the similarities with the handbills and computer messages of dubious origin that had been increasing in number since the night of June 4, he agreed with the anonymous editor in its cancellation. Some stories are beyond the comprehension of journalism; they belong to fiction.

Before leaving his office, Feng turned off the light on his desk, picked up the copy of this canceled dispatch and slipped it into his inside coat pocket where his bicycle key, a few coins and bits of aspirin had been accumulating, along with the other stories he had been working on recently.

Nine

ANOTHER KNOCKING on Sonny's door, and Madame Zhou stood there at its threshold more than an hour late looking very harassed and agitated.

"Sorry I am late," she said, coming in at once. "Barricades everywhere. Very serious. Soldiers at our conservatory compound gate ask for many IDs."

"Soldiers?" Sonny was surprised.

"Yes, two, with automatic rifles. I had to sign my name and give my address and occupation and show three IDs who I am."

The three of them sat down in the living room, and Madame Zhou spoke in whispers.

"Will there be trouble for you visiting an American today?" Sissy asked.

Sissy and Sonny had been listening to the BBC on his short-wave radio, and before the frequency was interrupted by high-pitched screeches, they had gathered that the student unrest had become startling international news, its coverage prompted by the world media coincidentally present in Beijing to cover Premier Mikhail Gorbachev's much-heralded state visit.

"I have been in trouble before," Madame Zhou answered. "They have been keeping an eye on me ever since I kept my job during cultural dissolution. Then I was in trouble because I was not doing anything. I was in trouble when I went to give recitals in America. Now I am in more trouble because I came back. What more trouble can another day bring?"

Sonny felt a heavy sympathy for Madame Zhou's position, and for just a moment imagined that he was talking with his own father, a chance he never had while he was still alive.

"You, Sonny, I want to know why you come to China?" Madame Zhou looked at Sonny carefully.

Sonny thought that the moment was too urgent to present his usual litany of reasons masking his real purpose in coming.

"I wanted to find out what had happened to the revolution that destroyed my father and made him — a rebel in his own profession — run away, a bitter and silent man living the rest of his life in an alien lie, like so many, many of his generation."

"Sorry Sonny. I did not know. When did he leave?"

"The last time? Nineteen forty-six."

"So he came back before then. The opposite of me. I left, but I came back; he came back and left for last time. And what did you find?"

"Nothing for sure," Sonny tried this one out, unsure of the answer. "Perhaps he could not buy into Mao, or Chiang for that matter. Perhaps he wanted to denounce them both and what they stood for by choosing to exile himself and his entire family too," but it didn't sound quite right to him.

"I mean," he continued, looking at Sissy, "it's easy to under-stand why he abhorred Chiang, but I'm not sure why he did not buy into Mao, at least the Mao of the thirties. Because he was an intellectual, he did not wish to condescend to low-life politics? Didn't he realize that the cannon-fodder's oppressed lives made his privilege? Don't you see, perhaps by not doing anything the intellectuals were asking for it? I still don't know, you see?"

"But there was so much optimism in Mao," Madame Zhou argued. "What confidence he had that the collective will of the people would rise up against boot of oppression and terror of conquest. A revolution."

"It is true," Sonny disregarded Madame Zhou's interrup-tion. He had to pursue his own logic. "It is true Mao had collected the people together to destroy the most obvious oppressors, the Japanese, the foreigners, the missionaries. Except for maybe Jesus, he had raised more people's conscious-ness and hope for longer than anyone else in history. But then what happened after that? Look at it now. The missionaries are back again. The foreign money is back again. The students are out protesting in the streets again, raising their fists against the exact same forms of oppression . . ."

"Yes, yes. I know, I know," impatient, Madame Zhou interrupted again.

". . . and maybe someone should have killed off Mao in 1949. Maybe it takes a different kind of person to put a nation together after a successful revolution than the kind that started it. But China did not have any potential candidate for that assassination — people like my father just packed up and quit, taking their families with them for Taiwan, for Hong Kong, for North or South America, occasionally playing a rueful DP's violin, giving a visiting dissident lecture at Brandeis, or accepting research grants from the CIA. I think the Red Guards in 1966 did not know that the totem they really wanted to knock off was Mao. They had misread history and killed those they imagined were opposed to him instead. Deng Xiaoping does not count, he's nothing more than a Western consumer terrorist. But the students out there, they had better know exactly what they're doing out there."

"And what will you do while all this is happening no more than a few hundred meters away," Madame Zhou asked Sonny, but she was looking at Sissy.

"Not knowing the language in a country in which I've only been a recent visitor for five months? My options are very limited. If I stayed, it would only be a symbolic but inconsequential and romantic gesture. There's been so much killing that nobody is blamed for it anymore. No one cares if anyone confesses that a mistake has been made. And besides, in fact I don't want to stay, or ever come back again. I am an American by birth, and anyone claiming that I'm Chinese hasn't looked closely enough. I am a foreigner here. Sissy and I have a place to go back to, our *home,* and we have our own political life to live there in Chicago. I have already made my closing statement here with my recital a month ago."

The light was diminishing in another late afternoon, and Sissy got up to turn on the lights, the three of them breathing in the silence of the apartment, and listening to the sound of sirens in the distance.

"And so you have accomplished purpose of your visit?" Madame Zhou finally asked.

"Well, yes in one part. The other I'm not so sure about, as you've heard. There doesn't seem to be any answer for what happened to my father, but the search itself has given me some new insights. And what about you? What will you do now?"

"I am not sure. I must do something," Madame Zhou looked away. "During cultural dissolution I turned my back and tried to move pianos by myself. I will not join other intellectuals and be moral but impotent onlookers; by what they are doing, these students have deprived my position of being observer. I am not that young anymore."

"And what do you think will happen?"

"I do not know. I only hope China will not kill its best again and dash our hope for dreams. Always the wrong ones getting killed. It seems that we have never known what to do with our disobedient children, our next generation, except to subjugate them to their parents' illusions, demolish their dreams, or banish or kill them."

They had all heard the heavy footsteps coming up the stairway. When Sonny responded to the loud and insistent knocking on his door, he opened it to the red-faced Georgetown law graduate from the American Embassy.

"Hi, you're the man from Grand Rapids, Michigan," Sonny tried to smile, but the official ignored it and walked right into the living room, eyeing Madame Zhou suspiciously.

"Mr. Ling, Miss George, you have exactly five minutes to pack one bag each," he said between breaths.

"What for?" Sissy asked.

"In case you haven't noticed, all hell's broken loose out there. We've been ordered to pick you two up and take you to the airport immediately. You must hurry."

"But today's Friday, the weekly United flight leaves on Thursdays," Sonny said.

"The States has chartered a 747 to evacuate the Americans in Beijing. Hurry, we haven't time."

"Can I make a phone call first to say goodbye?" Sissy asked.

"No. Pack now, the car's running outside."

Sonny looked over at Sissy, who nodded.

"Sorry, but we're not going with you," Sonny said.

"What? I can't order you. But if you stay, we can't give you any protection."

"We would rather take our chances getting out on our own than going with you," Sissy said.

"Okeydokey, have it your way, but don't say I didn't warn you," he said, and stomped down the stairs.

On their way down the stairs with their two bags stuffed with scores, passport and seals that had been given to them by Xiaomei, Sonny and Sissy felt themselves beginning to weep, but the only sound they heard were their footsteps leaving China and the wail of police sirens one heartbeat away.

Madame Zhou and Zheng Xiaomei accompanied Sonny and Sissy to the airport. As they pulled onto the Second Ring Road in the conservatory car, they noticed gathering crowds of people, most of them looking like students and intellectuals with their steadfast, serious look and trim clothes. At one corner they saw several groups of people collected together, arguing, some with raised fists, and a few carrying white wreaths and waving big-character red banners. There also seem to be more armed police gathered on the same corners. Sissy could see the intensity and agitation in some of the faces of those close to the street.

"What's going on here?" she asked.

"The respected Hu Yaobang died several days ago," Madame Zhou explained. "The students are also mourning his death."

"There is more," Xiaomei added. "There is more police now, armed police."

Sissy looked, and for the first time noticed that some of the policemen gathered at these street corners were wearing brown leather waist holsters.

"And over there, in the distance," Madame Zhou pointed, "that's where the students had gathered discussing waste and welfare in bureaucracy and corruption in party leadership, how government controls everything and does not trust its own people, just like old times."

"I have heard these students talk too," Xiaomei joined in. "This time I think perhaps students may be right. For these leaders, culture is a bottle of Nine Star beer and Panda cigarettes, and being driven in a curtained and chauffeured Red Flag limousine to a private showing of American films, or asking minority song-and-dance troupe to come to Beijing every year on National Day and do a dog-and-pony show for Premier Li Peng in the review stands on Tiananmen Square."

Sissy laughed out loud, and found it ironic that her friends, both musicians, were so intensely engaged in this political discussion. Back home their contemporaries would avoid participating in such referential issues, as if their musical language was above muddling in these low-life, day-to-day issues. She even remembered the story of the senior music professor at Indiana refusing to join in any of the 1960s demonstrations because he thought that academicians had to be politically neutral, thereby maintaining their objectivity and credibility.

But not these two, though Sissy noticed that both of them were using the third-person form of reporting in describing these events to her and Sonny, as if by reflex they'd slipped into a linguistic mode of distancing themselves from this political controversy and thereby reflecting an uninvolved personal position. But it was also clear to Sissy that their voices in this Beijing political spring had too much intensity that betrayed the neutrality of their words, as much as Sonny's silence, which she knew only meant that he was totally absorbing this entire discussion, or that he was saying his last *goodbye* to the China of his parents, or both.

While helping Zhiquan disappear, Sissy knew that she would be leaving soon, and that soon she would need to spend some time near the magic of her father's river and its healing stories, where place and description have tangible meanings, and where she would know the days by how the sun and the winds move, and the nights by the many voices coming up from the shadows of the water. For now, she had to say the difficult *goodbye* to what had moved her in China, the country inherited by her friend Xiaomei, a country with too much history.

Security at the airport was exceptionally tight and redundant. At the entrance doors, luggage and bags were X-rayed, and opened and searched, identifications demanded, and individuals bodily scanned and hand-searched, the entire process repeated fifty yards later.

"It's not the usual blue-uniformed airport police," Xiaomei observed. "And it is not the police. These dark-green uniforms belong to the Ministry of Public Security."

"The State has taken charge here," Madame Zhou added.

Xiaomei's and Madame Zhou's identifications were quickly approved, but they hesitated over Sissy's and Sonny's blue

American passports, considering the faces they belonged to. When they got to Sonny's booklet, the guard had to first ask for his superior's assistance for authentication before letting Sonny through.

It was unusually quiet inside the main terminal, and there were very few people other than passengers.

Sissy looked at her watch and turned to Xiaomei.

"We must go now," she said, giving her a generous hug.

"Goodbye Sissy," Madame Zhou said, hugging her too. "We will wait upstairs in the coffee shop," she pointed, "just until your flight leaves."

"Thank you Xiaomei, for asking me to do *Carmen*. I will never forget it."

Madame Zhou and Sonny shook hands, lingering.

"Sonny," Madame Zhou looked up at him. "Sonny, next time you come to Beijing, you can play your encore, Bach's *Goldberg.*"

"Perhaps."

"You go GREEN line."

So this has been their story.

In the last two years I have listened to each of them tell parts of it and have now faithfully reproduced them here without changing a word or substituting a metaphor, whenever possible.

Of course a few of the names have been changed or switched around to protect the innocent. But most of them have insisted on retaining their own names when I sent them their sections of the manuscript to check over for authenticity and if I'd left anything out or made something up.

There was a problem tracking down Professor Luo Zhi-quan however. Several weeks spent in Beijing in late 1991 failed to locate him. The career foreign service office from Grand Rapids, Michigan, was still assigned to the American Embassy, and he "Changchuned" me to a remote, cold city in north-east China on the rumored trail of Professor Luo. No one would admit having known him at Tsinghua. Xiaomei did mention she had heard the rumor that he had joined the disappeareds.

The rest of them? Well, I've kept their real names: sooner or later they'll have to be held accountable for the blood on their hands; sooner or later responsibility will have to be placed; sooner or later someone will have to admit to the tragic, irreversible mistakes.

This story about family of varying size set in the 1989 Beijing spring, ironically the fortieth anniversary of modern China's founding, has mapped the lives of those who have dared to resist the involuntary changes of space and place that have come to characterize the grand design of the twentieth century, such radical shifts in allegiance and location that will surely keep the political geographer occupied well into the twenty-first century. In so doing they have encountered the stultifying bureaucracies of tradition that have outlived their meaning, and the impoverished ideology's last hedge against any metaphor for voluntary change.

And whether or not I like it, it's also turned into a story about me, and you, whether or not you want to believe it.

About the author

In the middle of a professorial and administrative career, Alex Kuo went to teach American literature at a Beijing university in 1989, and as the Senior Fulbright Scholar at a key university in Changchun, China, in 1991–2.

As a writer, his poems, short stories, essays and articles have been widely published; his subjects have ranged from articles on bridge, economics and fundamentalist Christians, to stories on smokejumping and a group of school children terrorizing Beijing's Bank of China.

He was awarded a National Endowment for the Arts Fiction Fellowship in 1991 and United Nations and Idaho Commission for the Arts research grants to the Three Gorges Dam Project on the Yangtze River in 1994 to gather materials for his next novel. He is currently the Lingnan Visiting Scholar in American Studies at Hong Kong Baptist University and Hong Kong-America Center.

He has lived in the Palouse region of northern Idaho and eastern Washington for most of the last twenty years. Other books by Alex Kuo are *The Window Tree, New Letters from Hiroshima* and *Changing the River*.

Cheung Chau Dog Fanciers' Society
by Alan B Pierce

"A rare read indeed. Not only is it an accurate slice of Hong Kong life — touching on heroin smuggling, money laundering, corruption in the police force as well as in one of Hong Kong's most wealthy and powerful Chinese families — but it also depicts a very local journey of self-discovery. A superb description of insular life, complete with beery expatriates, ploddish village policemen, arm-wrestling triads and masses of day-trippers.

"A thriller with a difference." — **Hongkong Standard**

"One of the best Hong Kong novels ever written. It puts James Clavell to shame." — **HK Magazine**

"There are too few good novels set in Hong Kong's modern era. This is one of the better ones, with Pierce at his best when writing from the heart about the texture of life in a special place."
— **South China Morning Post**

ISBN 962-7160-38-5

Temutma
by Rebecca Bradley and John Stewart Sloan

Temutma, a *kuang-shi,* a monster similar to the vampire of European legend, is imprisoned beneath Kowloon Walled City in Hong Kong by his ancient keeper Wong San-bor. The monster escapes when the Walled City is being cleared for demolition. Hungering for blood it begins a horrifying series of murders, starting with the Ralston family on the Peak, saving only the daughter Julia for later enjoyment. A policeman, Scott, questions her, and as the deaths continue night after night comes to realise what he is pursuing — and is then pursuing him and Julia.

ISBN 962-7160-47-4

Hong Kong Rose

by Xu Xi

From a crumbling perch with a view of the Statue of Liberty, Rose Kho, Hong Kong girl who made it, lost it, and may be about to make it or lose it again, reflects, scotch in hand, on a life that "like an Indonesian mosquito disrupting my Chinese sleep" has controls of its own. Or, like a wounded fighter plane of the type her father used to fly, no controls at all. Xu Xi, the gifted, uncompromising storyteller, gives us a Hong Kong that sheds its artifice as a snake sheds its skin, only to grow new artifice. In Hong Kong Rose, petals metamorphose into scales that shine like mirror glass windows, reflecting equally the courage, cowardice and compromise of one of the world's great cities.

ISBN 962-7160-55-5

Riding a Tiger

The self-criticism of Arnold Fisher

by Robert Abel

A comic novel with a tragic twist, "written" by Arnold Fisher, as a deposition to the Chinese Ministry of Justice after he has been arrested and detained for immoral behaviour and building an illegal financial empire (trading in watermelons and bicycles, amongst other things) in Beijing and beyond, and his inadvertent involvement in the murder of a cadre. In the course of his self-criticism and interrogation he discovers who has betrayed him, and who he has betrayed in turn.

Robert Abel worked in Beijing as a foreign expert in 1987, when he was struck by the rebirth of the entrepreneurial spirit that is the basis of his story. He won the Flannery O'Connor Award for Short Fiction for his story "Ghost Traps".

ISBN 962-7160-50-4

Other titles
from
Asia 2000

Order from Asia 2000 Ltd
1101 Seabird House, 22–28 Wyndham St
Central, Hong Kong
tel (852) 2530 1409; fax (852) 2526 1107
email sales@asia2000.com.hk; http://www.asia2000.com.hk/